A TRIPLE TREAT OF

HORRID

HENRY

Francesca Simon

Illustrated by Tony Ross

Dolphin Paperbacks

Also by Francesca Simon

CONTENTS

First published in Great Britain in 2003
by Orion Children's Books
a division of the Orion Publishing Group Ltd
Orion House
5 Upper St Martin's Lane
London WC2H 9EA

Reprinted 2003, 2004 (three times)

ISBN 1 84255 250 3

A catalogue record for this book is
available from the British Library

Printed in Great Britain by
Clays Ltd, St Ives plc

www.orionbooks.co.uk

HORRiD HENRY

AND THE
MUMMY'S CURSE

For my friends and advisers,
Joe and Freddy Gaminara

CONTENTS

1

HORRID HENRY'S
HOBBY

"Out of my way, worm!" shrieked
Horrid Henry, pushing past his younger
brother Perfect Peter and dashing into
the kitchen.

"NO!" screamed Perfect Peter. He
scrambled after Henry and clutched
his leg.

"Get off me!" shouted Henry. He
grabbed the unopened Sweet Tweet
cereal box. "Nah nah ne nah nah,
I got it first."

Perfect Peter lunged for the Sweet
Tweet box and snatched it from Henry.
"But it's my turn!"

"No, mine!" shrieked Henry.

He ripped open the top and stuck his hand inside.

"It's mine!" shrieked Peter. He ripped open the bottom.

A small wrapped toy fell to the floor.

Henry and Peter both lunged for it.

"Gimme that!" yelled Henry.

"But it's my turn to have it!" yelled Peter.

"Stop being horrid, Henry!" shouted Mum. "Now give me that thing!"

Henry and Peter both held on tight.

"NO!" screamed Henry and Peter. "IT'S MY TURN TO HAVE THE TOY!"

Horrid Henry and Perfect Peter both collected Gizmos from inside Sweet Tweet cereal boxes. So did everyone at their school. There were ten different coloured Gizmos to collect, from the common green to the rare gold. Both Henry and Peter had Gizmos of every colour. Except for one. Gold.

"Right," said Mum, "whose turn is it to get the toy?"

"MINE!" screamed Henry and Peter.

"He got the last one!" screeched Henry. "Remember – he opened the new box and got the blue Gizmo."

It was true that Perfect Peter had got the blue Gizmo – two boxes ago. But why should Peter get any? If he hadn't started collecting Gizmos to copy me, thought Henry resentfully, I'd get every single one.

"NO!" howled Peter. He burst into tears. "Henry opened the last box."

"Cry-baby," jeered Henry.

"Stop it," said Peter.

"Stop it," mimicked Henry.

"Mum, Henry's teasing me," wailed Peter.

"I remember now," said Mum. "It's Peter's turn."

"Thank you, Mum," said Perfect Peter.

"It's not fair!" screamed Horrid Henry as Peter tore open the wrapping. There was a gold gleam.

"Oh my goodness," gasped Peter. "A gold Gizmo!"

Horrid Henry felt as if he'd been punched in the stomach. He stared at the glorious, glowing, golden Gizmo.

"It's not fair!" howled Henry. "I want a gold Gizmo!"

"I'm sorry, Henry," said Mum. "It'll be your turn next."

"But I want the gold one!" screamed
Henry.

He leaped on Peter and yanked the
Gizmo out of his hand. He was
Hurricane Henry uprooting everything
in his path.

"Hellllllllp!" howled Peter.

"Stop being horrid, Henry, or no more
Gizmos for you!" shouted Mum. "Now
clean up this mess and get dressed."

"NO!" howled Henry. He ran
upstairs to his room, slamming the door
behind him.

14

He had to have a gold Gizmo. He simply had to. No one at school had a gold one. Henry could see himself now, the centre of attention, everyone pushing and shoving just to get a look at his gold Gizmo. Henry could charge 20p a peek. Everyone would want to see it and to hold it. Henry would be invited to every birthday party. Instead, Peter would be the star attraction. Henry gnashed his teeth just thinking about it.

But how could he get one? You couldn't buy Gizmos. You could only get them inside Sweet Tweet cereal boxes. Mum was so mean she made Henry and Peter finish the old box before she'd buy a new one. Henry had eaten mountains of Sweet Tweet cereal to collect all his Gizmos. All that hard work would be in vain, unless he got a gold one.

He could, of course, steal Peter's. But

Peter would be sure to notice, and Henry would be the chief suspect.

He could swap. Yes! He would offer Peter *two* greens! That was generous. In fact, that was really generous. But Peter hated doing swaps. For some reason he always thought Henry was trying to cheat him.

And then suddenly Henry had a brilliant, spectacular idea. True, it did involve a little tiny teensy weensy bit of trickery, but Henry's cause was just. *He'd* been collecting Gizmos far longer than Peter had. He deserved a gold one, and Peter didn't.

"So, you got a gold Gizmo," said Henry, popping into Peter's room. "I'm really sorry."

Perfect Peter looked up from polishing his Gizmos. "Why?" he said suspiciously. "*Everyone* wants a gold Gizmo."

Horrid Henry looked sadly at Perfect Peter. "Not any more. They're very unlucky, you know. Every single person who's got one has died horribly."

Perfect Peter stared at Henry, then at his golden Gizmo.

"That's not true, Henry."

"Yes it is."

"No it isn't."

Horrid Henry walked slowly around Peter's room. Every so often he made a little note in a notebook.

"Marbles, check. Three knights, check. Nature kit – nah. Coin collection, check."

"What are you doing?" said Peter.

"Just looking round your stuff to see what I want when you're gone."

"Stop it!" said Peter. "You just made that up about gold Gizmos – didn't you?"

17

"No," said Henry. "It's in all the news-papers. There was the boy out walking his dog who fell into a pit of molten lava.

There was the girl who drowned in the loo, and then that poor boy who—"

"I don't want to die," said Perfect Peter. He looked pale. "What am I going to do?"

Henry paused. "There's nothing you can do. Once you've got it you're sunk."

Peter jumped up.

18

"I'll throw it away!"

"That wouldn't work," said Henry. "You'd still be jinxed. There's only one way out—"

"What?" said Perfect Peter.

"If you give the gold away to someone brave enough to take it, then the jinx passes to them."

"But no one will take it from me!" wailed Peter.

"Tell you what," said Henry. "I'll take the risk."

"Are you sure?" said Peter.

"Of course," said Horrid Henry. "You're my brother. You'd risk your life for me."

"OK," said Peter. He handed Henry the gold Gizmo. "Thank you, Henry. You're the best brother in the world."

"I know," said Horrid Henry.

He actually had his very own gold

Gizmo in his hand. It was his, fair and square. He couldn't wait to see Moody Margaret's face when he waved it in front of her. And Rude Ralph. He would be green with envy.

Then Perfect Peter burst into tears and ran downstairs.

"Mum!" he wailed. "Henry's going to die! And it's all my fault."

"What?" screeched Mum.

Uh oh, thought Henry. He clutched his treasure.

Mum stormed upstairs. She snatched the gold Gizmo from Henry.

"How could you be so horrid, Henry?" shouted Mum. "No TV for a week! Poor Peter. Now get ready. We're going shopping."

"NO!" howled Henry. "I'm not going!"

20

Horrid Henry scowled as he followed
Mum up and down the aisles of the
Happy Shopper. He'd crashed the cart
into some people so Mum wouldn't let
him push it. Then she caught him
filling the cart with crisps and fizzy
drinks and made him put them all back.
What a horrible rotten day this had
turned out to be.

"Yum, cabbage," said Perfect Peter. "Could we get some?"

"Certainly," said Mum.

"And beetroot, my favourite!" said Peter.

"Help yourself," said Mum.

"I want sweets!" screamed Henry.

"No," said Mum.

"I want doughnuts!" screamed Henry.

"No!" screamed Mum.

"There's nothing to eat here!" shrieked Henry.

"Stop being horrid, Henry," hissed Mum. "Everyone's looking."

"I don't care."

"Well I do," said Mum. "Now make yourself useful. Go and get a box of Sweet Tweets."

"All right," said Henry. Now was his chance to escape. Before Mum could stop him he grabbed a cart and

whizzed off.

"Watch out for the racing driver!" squealed Henry. Shoppers scattered as he zoomed down the aisle and screeched to a halt in front of the cereal section. There were the Sweet Tweets. A huge pile of them, in a display tower, under a twinkling sign saying, "A free Gizmo in every box! Collect them all!"

Henry reached for a box and put it in his cart.

And then Horrid Henry stopped. What was the point of buying a whole box if it just contained another green Gizmo? Henry didn't think he could bear it. I'll just check what's inside, he thought. Then, if it *is* a green one, I'll be prepared for the disappointment.

Carefully, he opened the box and slipped his hand inside. Aha! There was the toy. He lifted it out, and held it up to the light. Rats! A green Gizmo, just what he'd feared.

But wait. There was bound to be a child out there longing for a green Gizmo to complete his collection just as much as Henry was longing for a gold. Wouldn't it be selfish and horrid of Henry to take a green he didn't need when it would make someone else so happy?

I'll just peek inside one more box,

thought Horrid Henry, replacing the box
he'd opened and reaching for another.

Rip! He tore it open. Red.

Hmmm, thought Henry. Red is
surplus to requirements.

Rip! Another box opened. Blue.

Rip! Rip! Rip!

Green! Green! Blue!

I'll just try one more at the back, thought Henry. He stood on tiptoe, and stretched as far as he could. His hand reached inside the box and grabbed hold of the toy.

The tower wobbled.

CRASH!

Horrid Henry sprawled on the ground. Henry was covered in Sweet Tweets. So was the floor. So were all the shoppers.

"HELP!" screamed the manager, skidding in the mess. "Whose horrid boy is this?"

There was a very long silence.

"Mine," whispered Mum.

Horrid Henry sat in the kitchen surrounded by boxes and boxes and boxes of Sweet Tweets. He'd be eating Sweet Tweets for breakfast, lunch and dinner for weeks. But it was worth it, thought Henry happily. Banned for life from the Happy Shopper, how wonderful. He uncurled his hand to enjoy again the glint of gold.

Although he *had* noticed that Scrummy Yummies were offering a free Twizzle card in every box. Hmmmm, Twizzle cards.

2

HORRID HENRY'S HOMEWORK

Ahhhh, thought Horrid Henry. He turned on the TV and stretched out. School was over. What could be better than lying on the sofa all afternoon, eating crisps and watching TV? Wasn't life grand?

Then Mum came in. She did not look like a mum who thought life was grand. She looked like a mum on the warpath against boys who lay on sofas all afternoon, eating crisps and watching TV.

"Get your feet off the sofa, Henry!" said Mum.

"Unh," grunted Henry.

"Stop getting crisps everywhere!" snapped Mum.

"Unh," grunted Henry.

"Have you done your homework, Henry?" said Mum.

Henry didn't answer.

"HENRY!" shouted Mum.

"WHAT!" shouted Henry.

"Have you done your homework?"

"What homework?" said Henry. He kept his eyes glued to the TV.

"Go, Mutants!" he screeched.

"The five spelling words you are meant to learn tonight," said Mum.

"Oh," said Henry. "*That* homework."

Horrid Henry hated homework. He had far better things to do with his precious time than learn how to spell "zipper" or work out the answer to 6 x 7. For weeks Henry's homework sheets had ended up in the recycling box until Dad found them. Henry swore he had no idea how they got there and blamed

Fluffy the cat, but since then Mum and Dad had checked his school bag every day.

Mum snatched the zapper and switched off the telly.

"Hey, I'm watching!" said Henry.

"When are you going to do your homework, Henry?" said Mum.

"SOON!" screamed Henry. He'd just returned from a long, hard day at school. Couldn't he have any peace around here? When he was king anyone who said the word "homework" would get thrown to the crocodiles.

"I had a phone call today from Miss Battle-Axe," said Mum. "She said you got a zero in the last ten spelling tests."

"That's not *my* fault," said Henry. "First I lost the words, then I forgot, then I couldn't read my writing, then I copied the words wrong, then—"

"I don't want to hear any more silly excuses," said Mum. "Do you know your spelling words for tomorrow?"

"Yes," lied Henry.

"Where's the list?" Mum asked.

"I don't know," said Henry.

"Find it or no TV for a month," said Mum.

"It's not fair," muttered Henry, digging the crumpled spelling list out of his pocket.

Mum looked at it.

"There's going to be a test tomorrow," she said. "How do you spell 'goat'?"

"Don't you know how, Mum?" asked Henry.

"Henry. . ." said Mum.

Henry scowled.

"I'm busy," moaned Henry. "I promise I'll tell you right after Mutant Madman. It's my favourite show."

"How do you spell 'goat'?" said Mum.

"G-O-T-E," snapped Henry.

"Wrong," said Mum. "What about 'boat'?"

"Why do I have to do this?" wailed Henry.

"Because it's your homework," said Mum. "You have to learn how to spell."

"But why?" said Henry. "I never write letters."

"Because," said Mum. "Now spell "boat".

"B-O-T-T-E," said Henry.

"No more TV until you do your

33

homework," said Mum.

"I've done all *my* homework," said Perfect Peter. "In fact I enjoyed it so much I've already done tomorrow's homework as well."

Henry pounced on Peter. He was a cannibal tenderising his victim for the pot.

"Eeeeyowwww!" screamed Peter.

"Henry! Go to your room!" shouted Mum. "And don't come out until you know *all* your spelling words!"

Horrid Henry stomped upstairs and

34

slammed his bedroom door. This was so unfair! He was far too busy to bother with stupid, boring, useless spelling. For instance, he hadn't read the new Mutant Madman comic book. He hadn't finished drawing that treasure map. And he hadn't even begun to sort his new collection of Twizzle cards. Homework would have to wait.

There was just one problem. Miss Battle-Axe had said that everyone who spelled all their words correctly tomorrow would get a pack of Big Bopper sweets. Henry loved Big Bopper sweets. Mum and Dad hardly ever let him have them. But why on earth did he have to learn spelling words to get some? If *he* were the teacher, he'd only give sweets to children who couldn't spell. Henry sighed. He'd just have to sit down and learn those stupid words.

4:30. Mum burst into the room. Henry was lying on his bed reading a comic.

"Henry! Why aren't you doing your homework?" said Mum.

"I'll do it in a sec'," said Henry. "I'm just finishing this page."

"Henry . . ." said Mum.

Henry put down the comic.

Mum left. Henry picked up the comic.

5.30. Dad burst into the room. Henry was playing with his knights.

"Henry! Why aren't you doing your homework?" said Dad.

"I'm tired!" yawned Henry. "I'm just taking a little break. It's hard having so much work!"

"Henry, you've only got five words to learn!" said Dad. "And you've just spent two hours *not* learning them."

37

"All right," snarled Henry. Slowly, he picked up his spelling list. Then he put it down again. He had to get in the mood. Soothing music, that's what he needed. Horrid Henry switched on his cassette player. The terrible sound of the Driller Cannibals boomed through the house.

"OH, I'M A CAN-CAN-CANNI-BAL!" screamed Henry, stomping around his room. "DON'T CALL ME AN ANIMAL JUST 'CAUSE I'M A CAN-CAN-CANNIBAL!"

Mum and Dad stormed into Henry's bedroom and turned off the music.

"That's enough, Henry!" said Dad.

"DO YOUR HOMEWORK!" screamed Mum.

"IF YOU DON'T GET EVERY SINGLE WORD RIGHT IN YOUR TEST TOMORROW THERE WILL

BE NO TLEVISION FOR A WEEK!"
shouted Dad.

EEEK! No TV *and* no sweets! This was
too much. Horrid Henry looked at his
spelling words with loathing.

GOAT

BOAT

SAID

STOAT

FRIEND

"I hate goats! I'll never need to spell
the word 'goat' in my life," said Henry.
He hated goat's cheese. He hated goat's
milk. He thought goats were smelly. That

was one word he'd definitely never need to know.

The next word was "boat". Who needs to spell that, thought Henry. I'm not going to be a sailor when I grow up. I get sea-sick. In fact, it's bad for my health to learn how to spell 'boat'.

As for "said", what did it matter if he spelt it "sed"? It was perfectly under-standable, written "sed." Only an old fusspot like Miss Battle-Axe would mind such a tiny mistake.

Then there was "stoat". What on earth was a stoat? What a mean, sneaky word. Henry wouldn't know a stoat if it sat on him. Of all the useless, horrible words, "stoat" was the worst. Trust his teacher, Miss Battle-Axe to make him learn a horrible, useless word like stoat.

The last word was "friend". Well, a real friend like Rude Ralph didn't care how the word "friend" was spelt. As far as Henry was concerned any friend who minded how he spelt "friend" was no friend. Miss Battle-Axe included that word to torture him.

Five whole spelling words. It was too much. I'll never learn so many words, thought Henry. But what about tomorrow? He'd have to watch Moody Margaret and Jolly Josh and Clever Clare chomping away at those delicious Big Boppers, while he, Henry, had to gnash his empty teeth. Plus no TV for a week! Henry couldn't live that long without TV! He was sunk. He was doomed to be sweetless, and TV-less.

But wait. What if there was a way to get those sweets without the horrid hassle of learning to spell? Suddenly, Henry had a brilliant, spectacular idea. It was so simple Henry couldn't believe he'd never thought of it before.

He sat next to Clever Clare. Clare always knew the spelling words. All Henry had to do was to take a little peek at her work. If he positioned his chair right, he'd easily be able to see what she wrote. And he wouldn't be copying her, no way. Just double-checking. I am a genius, thought Horrid Henry. 100% right on the test. Loads of Big Bopper sweets. Mum and Dad would be so thrilled they'd let him watch extra TV. Hurray!

Horrid Henry swaggered into class the next morning. He sat down in his seat

between Clever Clare and Beefy Bert.
Carefully, he inched his chair over a
fraction so that he had a good view of
Clare's paper.

"Spelling test!" barked Miss Battle-
Axe. "First word – goat."

Clare bent over her paper. Henry
pretended he was staring at the wall,
then, quick as a flash, he glanced at her
work and wrote "goat".

"Boat," said Miss Battle-Axe. Again
Horrid Henry sneaked a look at Clare's
paper and copied her. And again.

And again.

This is fantastic, thought Henry. I'll never have to learn any spelling words. Just think of all the comic books he could read instead of wasting his time on homework! He sneaked a peek at Beefy Bert's paper. Blank. Ha ha, thought Henry.

There was only one word left. Henry could taste the tingly tang of a Big Bopper already. Wouldn't he swagger about! And no way would he share his sweets with anyone.

Suddenly, Clare shifted position and edged away from him. Rats! Henry couldn't see her paper any more.

"Last word," boomed Miss Battle-Axe. "Friend."

Henry twisted in his seat. He could see the first four words. He just needed to get a tiny bit closer . . .

Clare looked at him. Henry stared at the ceiling. Clare glared, then looked back at her paper. Quickly, Henry leaned over and . . . YES! He copied down the final word, "friend".

Victory!

Chomp! Chomp! Chomp! Hmmnn, boy, did those Big Boppers taste great!

Someone tapped him on the shoulder. It was Miss Battle-Axe. She was smiling at him with her great big yellow teeth.

Miss Battle-Axe had never smiled at Henry before.

"Well, Henry," said Miss Battle-Axe. "What an improvement! I'm thrilled."

"Thank you," said Henry modestly.

"In fact, you've done so well I'm promoting you to the top spelling group. Twenty-five extra words a night. Here's the list."

Horrid Henry's jaws stopped chomping. He looked in horror at the new spelling list. It was littered with words. But not just any words. Awful words. Mean words. Long words. HARD words.

Hieroglyphs.

Trapezium.

Diarrhoea.

"AAAAAHHHHHHHHHHHH!" shrieked Horrid Henry.

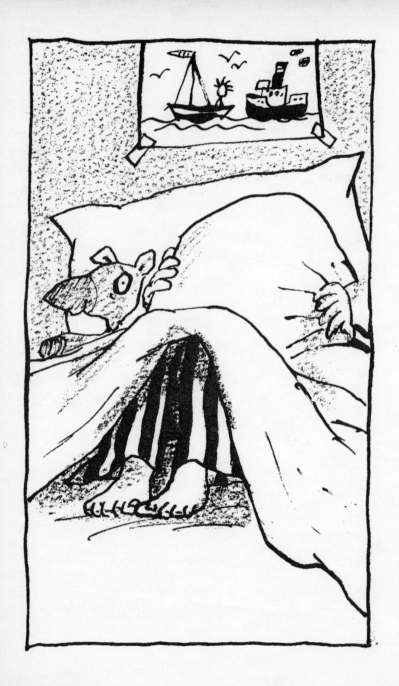

3

HORRID HENRY'S SWIMMING LESSON

Oh no! thought Horrid Henry. He pulled the duvet tightly over his head. It was Thursday. Horrible, horrible, Thursday. The worst day of the week. Horrid Henry was certain Thursdays came more often than any other day.

Thursday was his class swimming day. Henry had a nagging feeling that this Thursday was even worse than all the other awful Thursdays.

Horrid Henry liked the bus ride to the
pool. Horrid Henry liked doing the
dance of the seven towels in the changing
room. He also liked hiding in the lockers,
throwing socks in the pool, and splashing
everyone.

The only thing Henry didn't like

about going swimming was . . . swimming.

The truth was, Horrid Henry hated water. Ugggh! Water was so . . . wet! And soggy. The chlorine stung his eyes. He never knew what horrors might be lurking in the deep end. And the pool was so cold penguins could fly in for the winter.

Fortunately, Henry had a brilliant list of excuses. He'd pretend he had a verucca, or a tummy ache, or had lost his swimming costume. Unfortunately, the mean, nasty, horrible swimming teacher, Soggy Sid, usually made him get in the pool anyway.

Then Henry would duck Dizzy Dave, or splash Weepy William, or pinch Gorgeous Gurinder, until Sid ordered him out. It was not surprising that Horrid Henry had never managed to get his five-metre badge.

Arrrgh! Now he remembered. Today was test day. The terrible day when everyone had to show how far they could swim. Aerobic Al was going for gold. Moody Margaret was going for silver. The only ones who were still trying for their five-metre badges were Lazy Linda and Horrid Henry. Five whole metres! How could anyone swim such a vast distance?

If only they were tested on who could sink to the bottom of the pool the fastest, or splash the most, or spit water the furthest, then Horrid Henry would have every badge in a jiffy. But no. He had to leap into a freezing cold pool, and, if he survived that shock, somehow thrash his way across five whole metres without drowning.

Well, there was no way he was going to school today.

Mum came into his room.

"I can't go to school today, Mum," Henry moaned. "I feel terrible."

Mum didn't even look at him.

"Thursday-itis again, I presume," said Mum.

"No way!" said Henry. "I didn't even know it was Thursday."

"Get up Henry," said Mum. "You're going swimming and that's that."

Perfect Peter peeked round the door.

"It's badge day today!" he said. "I'm going for 50 metres!"

"That's brilliant, Peter," said Mum. "I bet you're the best swimmer in your class."

Perfect Peter smiled modestly.

"I just try my best," he said. "Good luck with your five-metre badge, Henry," he added.

Horrid Henry growled and attacked.

He was a Venus flytrap slowly mashing a frantic fly between his deadly leaves.

"Eeeeeowwww!" screeched Peter.

"Stop being horrid, Henry!" screamed Mum. "Leave your poor brother alone!"

Horrid Henry let Peter go. If only he could find some way not to take his swimming test he'd be the happiest boy in the world.

Henry's class arrived at the pool. Right, thought Henry. Time to unpack his excuses to Soggy Sid.

"I can't go swimming, I've got a verucca," lied Henry.

"Take off your sock," ordered Soggy Sid.

Rats, thought Henry.

"Maybe it's better now," said Henry.

"I thought so," said Sid.

Horrid Henry grabbed his stomach.

"Tummy pains!" he moaned. "I feel terrible."

"You seemed fine when you were prancing round the pool a moment ago," snapped Sid. "Now get changed."

Time for the killer excuse.

"I forgot my swimming costume!" said Henry. This was his best chance of success.

"No problem," said Soggy Sid. He handed Henry a bag. "Put on one of these."

Slowly, Horrid Henry rummaged in

the bag. He pulled out a bikini top, a
blue costume with a hole in the middle,
a pair of pink pants, a tiny pair of green
trunks, a polka-dot one piece with
bunnies, see-through white shorts, and
a nappy.

"I can't wear any of these!" protested
Horrid Henry.

"You can and you will, if I have to put
them on you myself," snarled Sid.

Horrid Henry squeezed into the green

trunks. He could barely breathe. Slowly, he joined the rest of his class pushing and shoving by the side of the pool.

Everyone had millions of badges sewn all over their costumes. You couldn't even see Aerobic Al's bathing suit beneath the stack of badges.

"Hey you!" shouted Soggy Sid. He pointed at Weepy William. "Where's your swimming costume?"

Weepy William glanced down and burst into tears.

"Waaaaah," he wailed, and ran weeping back to the changing room.

"Now get in!" ordered Soggy Sid.

"But I'll drown!" screamed Henry. "I can't swim!"

"Get in!" screamed Soggy Sid.

Goodbye, cruel world. Horrid Henry held his breath and fell into the icy water. ARRRRGH! He was turning into an iceberg!

He was dying! He was dead! His feet flailed madly as he sank down, down, down – clunk! Henry's feet touched the bottom.

Henry stood up, choking and spluttering. He was waist-deep in water.

"Linda and Henry! Swim five metres – now!"

What am I going to do? thought Henry. It was so humiliating not even being able to swim five metres! Everyone would tease him. And he'd have to listen to them bragging about their badges! Wouldn't it be great to get a badge? Somehow?

Lazy Linda set off, very very slowly. Horrid Henry grabbed on to her leg. Maybe she'll pull me across, he thought.

"Ugggh!" gurgled Lazy Linda.

"Leave her alone!" shouted Sid. "Last

chance, Henry."

Horrid Henry ran along the pool's bottom and flapped his arms, pretending to swim.

"Did it!" said Henry.

Soggy Sid scowled.

"I said swim, not walk!" screamed Sid. "You've failed. Now get over to the far lane and practise. Remember, anyone who stops swimming during the test doesn't get a badge."

Horrid Henry stomped over to the far lane. No way was he going to practise!

59

How he hated swimming! He watched
the others splashing up and down, up and
down. There was Aerobic Al, doing his
laps like a bolt of lightning. And Moody
Margaret. And Kung-Fu Kate. Everyone
would be getting a badge but Henry.
It was so unfair.

"Pssst, Susan," said Henry. "Have you
heard? There's a shark in the deep end!"

"Oh yeah, right," said Sour Susan. She
looked at the dark water in the far end of
the pool.

"Don't believe me," said Henry. "Find

out the hard way. Come back with a leg missing."

Sour Susan paused and whispered something to Moody Margaret.

"Shut up, Henry," said Margaret. They swam off.

"Don't worry about the shark, Andrew," said Henry. "I think he's already eaten today."

"What shark?" said Anxious Andrew.

Andrew stared at the deep end. It did look awfully dark down there.

"Start swimming, Andrew!" shouted Soggy Sid.

"I don't want to," said Andrew.

"Swim! Or I'll bite you myself!" snarled Sid.

Andrew started swimming.

"Dave, Ralph, Clare, and Bert – start swimming!" bellowed Soggy Sid.

"Look out for the shark!" said Horrid

Henry. He watched Aerobic Al tearing up and down the lane. "Gotta swim, gotta swim, gotta swim," muttered Al between strokes.

What a show-off, thought Henry. Wouldn't it be fun to play a trick on him?

Horrid Henry pretended he was a crocodile. He sneaked under the water to the middle of the pool and waited until Aerobic Al swam overhead. Then Horrid Henry reached up.

Pinch! Henry grabbed Al's thrashing leg.

"AAAARGGG!" screamed Al. "Something's grabbed my leg. Help!" Aerobic Al leaped out of the pool.

Tee hee, thought Horrid Henry.

"It's a shark!" screamed Sour Susan. She scrambled out of the pool.

"There's a shark in the pool!" screeched Anxious Andrew.

"There's a shark in the pool!" howled Rude Ralph.

Everyone was screaming and shouting and struggling to get out.

The only one left in the pool was Henry.

Shark!

Horrid Henry forgot there were no sharks in swimming pools.

Horrid Henry forgot *he'd* started the shark rumour.

Horrid Henry forgot he couldn't swim.

All he knew was that he was alone in the pool – with a shark!

Horrid Henry swam for his life.

Shaking and quaking, splashing and
crashing, he torpedoed his way to the
side of the pool and scrambled out.
He gasped and panted. Thank goodness.
Safe at last! He'd never ever go
swimming again.

"Five metres!" bellowed Soggy Sid.

"You've all failed your badges today, except for – Henry!"

"Waaaaaaahhhhhh!" wailed the other children.

"Whoopee!" screamed Henry. "Olympics, here I come!"

4

HORRID HENRY
AND THE
MUMMY'S CURSE

Tiptoe. Tiptoe. Tiptoe.

Horrid Henry crept down the hall.
The coast was clear. Mum and Dad were
in the garden, and Peter was playing at
Tidy Ted's.

Tee hee, thought Henry, then darted
into Perfect Peter's room and shut the
door.

There it was. Sitting unopened on
Peter's shelf. The grossest, yuckiest, most
stomach-curdling kit Henry had ever
seen. A brand-new, deluxe "Curse of the
Mummy" kit, complete with a plastic
body to mummify, mummy-wrapping

gauze, curse book, amulets and, best of all, removable mummy organs to put in a canopic jar. Peter had won it at the "Meet a Real Mummy" exhibition at the museum, but he'd never even played with it once.

Of course, Henry wasn't allowed into Peter's bedroom without permission. He was also not allowed to play with Peter's toys. This was so unfair, Henry could hardly believe it. True, he wouldn't let Peter touch his Boom-Boom Basher, his Goo-Shooter, or his Dungeon Drink kit. In fact, since Henry refused to share *any*

of his toys with Peter, Mum had forbidden
Henry to play with any of Peter's toys – or
else.

Henry didn't care – Perfect Peter had
boring baby toys – until, that is, he
brought home the mummy kit. Henry had
ached to play with it. And now was his
chance.

Horrid Henry tore off the wrapping,
and opened the box.

WOW! So gross! Henry felt a delicious
shiver. He loved mummies. What could be
more thrilling than looking at an ancient,
wrapped-up DEAD body? Even a pretend
one was wonderful. And now he had
hours of fun ahead of him.

Pitter-patter! Pitter-patter! Pitter-patter!

Oh help, someone was coming up the
stairs! Horrid Henry shoved the mummy
kit behind him as Peter's bedroom door
swung open and Perfect Peter strolled in.

"Out of my way, worm!" shouted Henry.

Perfect Peter slunk off. Then he stopped.

"Wait a minute," he said. "You're in *my* room! You can't order me out of my own room!"

"Oh yeah?" blustered Henry.

"Yeah!" said Peter.

"You're supposed to be at Ted's," said Henry, trying to distract him.

"He got sick," said Peter. He stepped closer. "And you're playing with my kit! You're not allowed to play with any of

70

my things! Mum said so! I'm going to tell her right now!"

Uh oh. If Peter told on him Henry would be in big trouble. Very big trouble. Henry had to save himself, fast. He had two choices. He could leap on Peter and throttle him. Or he could use weasel words.

"I wasn't playing with it," said Henry smoothly. "I was trying to protect you."

"No you weren't," said Peter. "I'm telling."

"I was, too," said Henry. "I was trying to protect you from the Mummy's Curse."

Perfect Peter headed for the door. Then he stopped.

"What curse?" said Peter.

"The curse which turns people into mummies!" said Henry desperately.

"There's no such thing," said Peter.

71

"Wanna bet?" said Henry. "Everyone knows about the mummy's curse! They take on the shape of someone familiar but really, they're mummies! They could be your cat—"

"Fluffy?" said Peter. "Fluffy, a mummy?"

Henry looked at fat Fluffy snoring peacefully on a cushion.

"Even Fluffy," said Henry. "Or Dad. Or Me. Or you."

"I'm not a mummy," said Peter.

"Or even—" Henry paused melodramatically and then whispered, "Mum."

"Mum, a mummy?" gasped Peter.

"Yup," said Henry. "But don't worry. You help me draw some Eyes of Horus. They'll protect us against . . . her."

"She's not a mummy," said Peter.

"That's what she wants us to think," whispered Henry. "It's all here in the Mummy curse book." He waved the book in front of Peter. "Don't you think the mummy on the cover resembles you-know-who?"

"No," said Peter.

"Watch," said Horrid Henry. He grabbed a pencil.

73

"Don't draw on a book!" squeaked Peter.

Henry ignored him and drew glasses on the mummy.

"How about now?" he asked.

Peter stared. Was it his imagination or did the mummy look a little familiar?

"I don't believe you," said Peter. "I'm going straight down to ask Mum."

"But that's the worst thing you could do!" shouted Henry.

"I don't care," said Peter. Down he went.

Henry was sunk. Mum would probably cancel his birthday party when Peter blabbed. And he'd never even had a chance to play with the mummy kit! It was so unfair.

Mum was reading on the sofa.

"Mum," said Peter, "Henry says you're a mummy."

Mum looked puzzled.

"Of course I'm a mummy," she said.

"What?" said Peter.

"I'm your mummy," said Mum, with a smile.

Peter took a step back.

"I don't want you to be a mummy," said Peter.

"But I am one," said Mum. "Now come and give me a hug."

"No!" said Peter.

75

"Let me wrap my arms around you," said Mum.

"NO WRAPPING!" squealed Peter. "I want my mummy!"

"But I'm your mummy," said Mum.

"I know!" squeaked Peter. "Keep away, you . . . Mummy!"

Perfect Peter staggered up the stairs to Henry.

"It's true," he gasped. "She said she was a mummy."

"She did?" said Henry.

"Yes," said Peter. "What are we going to do?"

"Don't worry, Peter," said Henry. "We can free her from the curse."

"How?" breathed Peter.

Horrid Henry pretended to consult the curse book.

"First we must sacrifice to the Egyptian gods Osiris and Hroth," said Henry.

"Sacrifice?" said Peter.

"They like cat guts, and stuff like that," said Henry.

"No!" squealed Peter. "Not . . . Fluffy!"

"However," said Henry, leafing through the curse book, "marbles are also acceptable as an offering."

Perfect Peter ran to his toybox and scooped up a handful of marbles.

"Now fetch me some loo roll," added Henry.

"Loo roll?" said Peter.

"Do not question the priest of Anubis!" shrieked Henry.

Perfect Peter fetched the loo roll.

"We must wrap Fluffy in the sacred bandages," said Henry. "He will be our messenger between this world and the next."

"Meoww," said Fluffy, as he was wrapped from head to tail in loo paper.

"Now you," said Henry.

78

"Me?" squeaked Peter.

"Yes," said Henry. "Do you want to free Mum from the mummy's curse?"

Peter nodded.

"Then you must stand still and be quiet for thirty minutes," said Henry. That should give him plenty of time to have a go with the mummy kit.

He started wrapping Peter. Round and round and round and round went the loo roll until Peter was tightly trussed from head to toe.

Henry stepped back to admire his work. Goodness, he was a brilliant mummy-maker! Maybe that's what he should be when he grew up. Henry, the Mummy-Maker. Henry, World's Finest Mummy-Maker. Henry, Mummy-Maker to the Stars. Yes, it certainly had a ring to it.

"You're a fine-looking mummy, Peter," said Henry. "I'm sure you'll be made very welcome in the next world."

"Huuunh?"said Peter.

"Silence!"ordered Henry. "Don't move. Now I must utter the sacred spell. By the powers of Horus, Morus, Borus and Stegosaurus," intoned Henry, making up all the Egyptian sounding names he could.

"Stegosaurus?" mumbled Peter.

"Whatever!" snapped Henry. "I call on the scarab! I call on Isis! Free Fluffy from the mummy's curse. Free Peter from the mummy's curse. Free Mum from the mummy's curse. Free— "

"What on earth is going on in here?" shrieked Mum, bursting through the door. "You horrid boy! What have you done to Peter? And what have you done to poor Fluffy?"

"Meoww," yowled Fluffy.

"Mummy!" squealed Perfect Peter.

Eowww, gross! thought Horrid Henry, opening up the plastic mummy body and placing the organs in the canopic jar.

The bad news was that Henry had been banned from watching TV for a week. The good news was that Perfect Peter had said he never wanted to see that horrible mummy kit again.

HORRID HENRY'S
REVENGE

For Chris Harris, Wendy Kinnard,
Ben, Sophie and Jessica with love

CONTENTS

1

HORRID HENRY'S REVENGE

SLAP!

"Waaaaaaaaaa!"

SLAP! SLAP! PINCH!

"Muuuummmmmm!" shrieked Peter. "Henry slapped me!"

"Did not!"

"Did too! And he pinched me!"

"Stop being horrid, Henry!" said Mum.

"But Peter started it!" shouted Henry.

"Did not!" wailed Peter. "Henry did!"

Horrid Henry glared at Perfect Peter.

Perfect Peter glared at Horrid Henry.

Mum went back to writing her letter. Horrid Henry lashed out and pulled Peter's hair. He was a coiling cobra unleashing his venom.

"Eowwwwww!" shrieked Peter.

"Go to your room, Henry!" screamed Dad. "I've had just about enough of you today!"

"Fine!" shouted Henry. "I hate you, Peter!" he shrieked, stomping up to his bedroom and slamming the door as loud as he could.

It was so unfair! Peter was never sent to his room. Horrid Henry was sent to *his* so often he might as well live there full-time. Henry couldn't burp without Peter trying to get him into trouble.

"Mum! Henry's dropping peas on the floor!"

"Dad! Henry's sneaking sweets!"

"Mum! Henry's eating on the new sofa!"

"Dad! Henry's playing on the phone!"

Horrid Henry had had enough. He was sick and tired of that goody-goody ugly toad tattle-tale brat.

But what could he do about Peter? He'd tried selling him as a slave to Moody Margaret, but Henry didn't think she'd buy him again. If only he knew how to cast spells, he could turn Peter into a toad or a beetle or a worm. Yes! Wouldn't that be great! He'd charge everyone 10p to look at his brother, the worm. And if Peter-worm *ever* wriggled out of line he'd be fish bait. Horrid Henry smiled.

Then he sighed. The truth was, he was stuck with Peter. But if he couldn't sell Peter, and he couldn't turn Peter into a worm, he *could* get Peter into trouble.

Unfortunately, getting Perfect Peter into trouble was easier said than done. Peter never did anything wrong. Also, for some reason he didn't always trust Henry. The only way to get Peter into trouble was to trick him. And if it took all year, Horrid Henry vowed he would come up with a perfect plan. A plan to get Peter into trouble. Big, big, BIG trouble. That would be almost as good as turning him into a worm.

"I'll pay you back, Peter," growled Henry, thumping his teddy, Mr Kill, against the bedpost. "I will be revenged on you!"

"What are you doing, Henry?" asked Peter.

"Nothing," said Horrid Henry. Quickly he stopped poking around the old apple tree at the end of the garden and stood up.

"You're doing something, I know you are," said Peter.

"Whatever I'm doing is none of your business, telltale," said Henry.

"Have you found something?" said Peter. He looked at the base of the tree. "I don't see anything."

"Maybe," said Henry. "But I'm not telling you. You can't keep a secret."

"Yes I can," said Peter.

"And you're too young," said Henry.

"No I'm not," said Peter. "I'm a big boy. Mum said so."

"Well, too bad," said Horrid Henry. "Now go away and leave me alone. I'm doing something important."

Perfect Peter slunk off about ten paces, then turned and stood still, watching Henry.

Horrid Henry continued to prowl around the tree, staring intently at the grass. Then he whistled and dropped to his knees.

"What have you found?" said Perfect Peter eagerly. "Treasure?"

"Much better than treasure," said Horrid Henry. He picked something up and hid it in his hand.

"Oh show me," said Peter. "Please. Oh please!"

Horrid Henry considered.

"If – and I mean if – I tell you something, do you swear by the sacred oath of the purple hand to say nothing about this to anyone?"

"I swear," said Peter.

"Even if you're being tortured by aliens?"

"I WON'T TELL!" shrieked Peter.

Horrid Henry put his finger to his lips, then tiptoed away from the tree to his fort. Peter followed.

"I don't want them to know I'm telling you," he whispered, when they

95

were hidden behind the branches.
"Otherwise they'll disappear."

"Who?" whispered Peter.

"The fairies," said Henry.

"Fairies," squeaked Perfect Peter. "You
mean you've seen—"

"Shh!" hissed Horrid Henry. "They'll
run away if you tell anyone."

"I won't," said Perfect Peter. "Promise.
Oh wow, fairies! In our garden! Oh,
Henry! Fairies! Just wait till I tell my
teacher."

"NO!" screamed Horrid Henry. "Tell
no one. Especially grown-ups. Fairies
hate grown-ups. Grown-ups stink to
fairies."

Perfect Peter clasped his hand over his
mouth.

"Sorry, Henry," he said.

Horrid Henry opened his hand. It was
sprinkled with gold glitter.

"Fairy dust," said Horrid Henry.

"It looks just like glitter," said Perfect Peter.

"Of course it looks like glitter," said Horrid Henry. "Where do you think glitter comes from?"

"Wow," said Peter. "I never knew glitter came from fairies."

"Well now you know," said Henry.

"Can I see them, Henry?" asked Peter.

"Please let me see them!"

"They only come out to dance at dead of night," said Horrid Henry.

"Past my bedtime?" said Perfect Peter.

"'Course," said Horrid Henry. "Midnight is the fairy hour."

"Oh," said Peter. His face fell.

"Told you you were too young," said Henry.

"Wait," said Perfect Peter. "If they only come out at midnight, how come *you've* seen them?"

"Because I've sneaked out and hidden up the apple tree," said Horrid Henry. "It's the only way."

"Ah," said Perfect Peter. "Umm," said Perfect Peter. "Ooh," said Perfect Peter.

"I'm going to see them tonight," said Henry casually.

"Do you think you could ask them to come before seven thirty?" said Peter.

"Oh yeah, right," said Henry. "Hiya, fairies! My brother wants you to dance for him at seven o'clock." "Sure thing, Henry," said Henry in a high squeaky fairy voice. "You don't speak to fairies. You have to hide up the tree. If they knew I'd seen them they'd run away and never come back."

Perfect Peter was in torment. He wanted to see the fairies more than anything in the world. But getting out of bed after lights out! And sneaking outside! And climbing the tree! And on a school night! It was too much.

"I can't do it," whispered Perfect Peter.

Henry shrugged. "Fine, baby. You need your rest."

Peter hated being called baby. Next to "smelly nappy", it was the worst name Henry could call him.

"I am not a baby."

"Yes you are," said Henry. "Now go away, baby. Just don't blame me when you spend the rest of your life moaning that you missed seeing real live fairies."

Horrid Henry started to leave the fort.

Perfect Peter sat very still. Fairies! But was he brave enough, and bad enough, to sneak out of the house – at night?

"Don't do it," whispered his angel.

"Do it," squeaked his devil, a very small, sad, puny creature who spent his life inside Peter's head squashed flat by the angel.

"I'll come," said Perfect Peter.

YES! thought Horrid Henry.

"Okay," said Henry.

Tiptoe. Tiptoe. Tiptoe.

Tiptoe. Tiptoe. Tiptoe.

Horrid Henry sneaked down the stairs. Perfect Peter followed him. Softly, Henry opened the back door, and slipped outside. He held a small torch.

"It's so dark!" said Perfect Peter, staring into the shadows at the bottom of the garden.

"Quiet," whispered Horrid Henry. "Follow me."

They crept across the lawn down to the apple tree.

Perfect Peter looked up into the ghostly branches.

"It's too high for me to climb," he protested.

"No it isn't, I'll give you a leg up," said Horrid Henry. He grabbed Peter and shoved him up. Peter caught the lowest branch and started to climb.

"Higher," said Henry. "Go as high as you can."

Peter climbed. And climbed. And climbed.

"This is high enough," squeaked Perfect Peter. He settled himself on a branch, then cautiously looked down. "I don't see anything," he whispered.

There was no reply.

"Henry?" said Peter.

"Henry!" said Peter, a little louder.

Still there was no reply. Perfect Peter peered into the darkness. Where could he be? Could Henry have been kidnapped by fairies? Oh no!

Then Perfect Peter saw a dreadful sight.

There was his brother, darting back into the house!

Perfect Peter did not understand. Why wasn't Henry waiting to see the fairies? Why had he left Peter?

And then suddenly Peter realised the terrible truth. His treacherous brother had tricked him.

"I'll get you – you're gonna be in big trouble – I'll – I'll – " squeaked Peter. Then he stopped. His legs were too short to reach the lower branch.

Perfect Peter couldn't climb down. He was stuck up a tree, all alone, at night. He had three choices. He could wait and hope that Henry would come back and help him. Fat chance. Or he could sleep all night in the damp, cold, scary, spooky tree. Or he could—

"MUUUUUUUM!" screamed Peter.

"DAAAADD!"

Mum and Dad stumbled out into the darkness. They were furious.

"What are you doing out here, Peter!" screamed Mum.

"You horrible boy!" screamed Dad.

"It was Henry's fault!" shrieked Peter, as Dad helped him down. "He brought me here! He made me climb up."

"Henry is sound asleep in bed," said Mum. "We checked on the way out."

"I am so disappointed in you, Peter," said Dad. "No stamp collecting for a month."

"WAAAAAAAH!" wailed Peter.

"Shuddup!" screamed the neighbours. "We're trying to sleep."

Meanwhile, back in bed, Horrid Henry stretched and smiled. No one could pretend to be asleep better than Horrid Henry.

What a perfect revenge, he thought. Peter in trouble. Henry in the clear. He was so excited he never noticed his torn, dirty, leafy pyjamas.

Unfortunately, the next morning, Mum did.

2

HORRID HENRY'S COMPUTER

"No, no, no, no, no!" said Dad.

"No, no, no, no, no!" said Mum.

"The new computer is only for work," said Dad. "My work, Mum's work, and school work."

"Not for playing silly games," said Mum.

"But everyone plays games on their computer," said Henry.

"Not in this house," said Dad. He looked at the computer and frowned. "Hmmn," he said. "How do you turn this thing off?"

"Like this," said Horrid Henry. He pushed the "off" button.

"Aha," said Dad.

It was so unfair! Rude Ralph had Intergalactic Robot Rebellion. Dizzy Dave had Snake Masters Revenge III. Moody Margaret had Zippy Zappers. Horrid Henry had Be a Spelling Champion, Virtual Classroom, and Whoopee for Numbers. Aside from Beefy Bert, who'd been given Counting Made Easy for Christmas, no one else had such awful software.

"What's the point of finally getting a computer if you can't play games?" said Horrid Henry.

"You can improve your spelling," said Perfect Peter. "And write essays. I've already written one for school tomorrow."

"I don't want to improve my

spelling!" screamed Henry. "I want to play games!"

"I don't," said Perfect Peter. "Unless it's "Name that Vegetable" of course."

"Quite right, Peter," said Mum.

"You're the meanest parents in the world and I hate you," shrieked Henry.

"You're the best parents in the world and I love you," said Perfect Peter.

Horrid Henry had had enough. He leapt on Peter, snarling. He was the Loch Ness monster gobbling up a thrashing duck.

"OWWWWWW!" squealed Peter.

"Go to your room, Henry!" shouted Dad. "You're banned from the computer for a week."

"We'll see about that," muttered Horrid Henry, slamming his bedroom door.

Snore. Snore. Snore.

Horrid Henry sneaked past Mum and Dad's room and slipped downstairs.

There was the new computer. Henry sat down in front of it and looked longingly at the blank screen.

How could he get some games? He had 53p saved up. Not even enough for Snake Masters Revenge I, he thought miserably. Everyone he knew had fun on their computers. Everyone except him. He loved zapping aliens. He loved marshalling armies. He loved ruling the world. But no. His yucky parents would only let him have educational games. Ugh. When he was king anyone who wrote an educational game would be fed to the lions.

Horrid Henry sighed and switched on the computer. Maybe some games were hidden on the hard disk, he thought hopefully. Mum and Dad were scared of computers and wouldn't know how to look.

The word "Password" flashed up on the screen.

I know a good password, thought Horrid Henry. Quickly he typed in "Smelly Socks".

113

Then Horrid Henry searched. And searched. And searched. But there were no hidden games. Just boring stuff like Mum's spreadsheets and Dad's reports.

Rats, thought Henry. He leaned back in the chair. Would it be fun to switch around some numbers in Mum's dreary spreadsheet? Or add a few words like "yuck" and "yah, boo, you're a ninny," to Dad's stupid report?

Not really.

Wait, what was this? Perfect Peter's homework essay!

Let's see what he's written, thought Henry. Perfect Peter's essay appeared on the screen, titled, "Why I love my teacher".

Poor Peter, thought Henry. What a boring title. Let's see if I can improve it for him.

Tap tap tap.

Peter's essay was now called, "Why I hate my teacher."

That's more like it, thought Henry. He read on.

```
"My teacher is the best. She's
kind, she's fun, and she makes
learning a joy. I am so lucky to
be in Miss Lovely's class. Hip hip
hooray for Miss Lovely."
```

Oh dear. Worse and worse, thought Horrid Henry. Tap tap tap.

"My teacher is the worst." Still missing something, thought Henry.

Tap tap.

"My fat teacher is the worst."

That's more like it, thought Henry. Now for the rest.

Tap tap tap tap tap.

"My fat teacher is the worst. She's mean, she's horrible, and she makes learning a misery. I am so unlucky to be in Miss Ugly's class. Boo hiss for Miss Ugly."

Much better.

Now that's what I call an essay, thought Horrid Henry. He pressed "Save", then switched off the computer and tiptoed back to bed.

"ARRRGGHHHH!"

"AAAHHHH!"

"NOOOOO!"

Horrid Henry jumped out of bed. Mum was shrieking. Dad was shrieking. Peter was shrieking.

Honestly, couldn't anyone get any rest around here? He stomped down the stairs.

Everyone was gathered round the computer.

"Do something!" shouted Dad. "I need that report now."

"I'm trying!" shouted Mum. She pressed a few keys.

117

"It's jammed," she said.

"My essay!" wailed Perfect Peter.

"My spreadsheet!" wailed Mum.

"My report!" wailed Dad.

"What's wrong?" said Henry.

"The computer's broken!" said Dad.

"How I hate these horrible machines," said Mum.

"You've got to fix it," said Dad. "I've got to hand in my report this morning."

"I can't," said Mum. "The computer won't let me in."

"I don't understand," said Dad. "We've never needed a password before."

Suddenly Horrid Henry realised what was wrong. He'd set a new password. No one could use the computer without it. Mum and Dad didn't know anything about passwords. All Horrid Henry had to do to fix the computer was to type in

118

the password "Smelly Socks."

"I might be able to help, Dad," said Horrid Henry.

"Really?" said Dad. He looked doubtful.

"Are you sure?" said Mum. She looked doubtful.

"I'll try," said Horrid Henry. He sat down in front of the computer. "Whoops, no I can't," said Horrid Henry.

"Why not?" said Mum.

"I'm banned," said Henry. "Remember?"

"All right, you're unbanned," said Dad, scowling. "Just hurry up."

"I have to be at school with my essay in ten minutes!" moaned Peter.

"And I have to get to work!" moaned Mum.

"I'll do my best," said Horrid Henry slowly. "But this is a very hard problem to solve."

He tapped a few keys and frowned at the screen.

"Do you know what's wrong, Henry?" asked Dad.

"The hard disk is disconnected from the harder disk, and the hardest disk has slipped," said Horrid Henry.

"Oh," said Dad.

"Ahh," said Mum.

"Huunh?" said Perfect Peter.

"You learn about that stuff in computer class next year," said Horrid Henry. "Now stand back, everyone, you're making me nervous."

Mum, Dad, and Peter stepped back.

"You're our last hope, Henry," said Mum.

"I will fix this on one condition, " said Henry.

"Anything," said Dad.

"Anything," said Mum.

"Deal," said Horrid Henry, and typed in the password.

Whirr! Whirr! Spit! Horrid Henry scooped up Mum's spreadsheet, Dad's report, and Perfect Peter's essay from the printer and handed them round.

"Thank you so much," said Dad.
"Thank you so much," said Mum.

Perfect Peter beamed at his beautifully printed essay, then put it carefully into his school bag. He'd never handed in a printed essay before. He couldn't wait to see what Miss Lovely said.

"Oh my goodness, Peter, what a smart looking essay you've written!" said Miss Lovely.

"It's all about you, Miss Lovely," said Peter, beaming. "Would you like to read it?"

"Of course," said Miss Lovely. "I'll read it to the class."

She cleared her throat and began:

"Why I ha—" Miss Lovely stopped reading. Her face went pink. "Peter!" she gasped. "Go straight to the head! Now!"

"But – but – is it because my essay is so good?" squeaked Peter.

"NO!" said Miss Lovely.

"Waaaaahhh!" wailed Perfect Peter.

PEEEEOWWWW! BANG! RAT-A-
TAT- TAT! Another intergalactic robot
bit the dust. Now, what shall I play next?
thought Horrid Henry happily. Snake
Masters Revenge lll? Zippy Zapper?
Best of all, Perfect Peter had been banned

from the computer for a week, after Miss
Lovely had phoned Mum and Dad to tell
them about Peter's rude essay. Peter
blamed Henry. Henry blamed the
computer.

3

HORRID HENRY
GOES TO WORK

"It's your turn!"

"No, it's yours!"

"Yours!"

"Yours!"

"I took Henry last year!" said Mum.

Dad paused. "Are you sure?"

"YES," said Mum.

"Are you sure you're sure?" said Dad.
He looked pale.

"Of course I'm sure!" said Mum.
"How could I forget?"

Tomorrow was take your child to

work day'. Mum wanted to take Peter. Dad wanted to take Peter. Unfortunately, someone had to take Henry.

Only today Dad's boss had said how much he was looking forward to meeting Dad's lovely son. "Of course I'll be bringing my boy, Bill," said Big Boss. "He's a great kid. Good as gold. Smart as a whip. Superb footballer. Brilliant at maths. Plays trumpet like a genius. Perfect manners. Yep, I sure am proud of Bill."

Dad tried not to hate Bill. He failed.

"Now listen, Henry," said Dad. "You're coming to work with me tomorrow. I'm warning you, my boss is bringing *his* son. From what I hear he's perfect."

"Like me?" said Peter. "I'd love to meet him. We could swap good deed ideas! Do you think he'd like to join my Best Boys Club?"

"You're going to Mum's work," said Dad sadly. "I'm taking Henry."

"Cool!" said Henry. A day out of school! A day at the office! "I want to play computer games. And eat doughnuts! And surf the web!"

"NO!" said Dad. "An office is a place where people work. I want perfect behaviour. My boss is very strict. Don't let me down, Henry."

"Of course I won't," said Horrid Henry. He was outraged. How could Dad think such a thing? The only trouble was, how could Henry have any fun with a boring goody-goody like Bill around?

"Remember what I said, Henry," said Dad the next morning, as they arrived at his office. "Be nice to Bill. Do what he says. He's the boss's son. Try to be as good as he is."

"All right," said Henry sourly.

Dad's boss came to welcome them.

"Ah, you must be Henry!" said Big Boss. "This is my son, Bill."

"So pleased to meet you, Henry," said Bossy Bill.

"Huh," grunted Horrid Henry.

He looked at Bossy Bill. He was wearing a jacket and tie. His face was gleaming. His shoes were so polished Henry could see his dirty face in them. Just his luck to get stuck all day with boring old Bossy Bill.

"Right, boys, your first job is to make tea for everyone in the meeting room," said Big Boss.

"Do I have to?" said Horrid Henry.

"Henry!" said Dad.

"Yes," said Big Boss. "That's six teas, one sugar in each."

"Gee thanks, Dad!" said Bossy Bill. "I love making tea."

"Whoopee," muttered Horrid Henry.

Big Boss beamed and left the room. Horrid Henry was alone with Bossy Bill.

The moment Big Boss left, Bill's face changed.

"Why doesn't he make his own stupid tea!" he snarled.

"I thought you loved making tea," said Horrid Henry. Maybe things were looking up.

"No way," said Bossy Bill. "What am I, a servant? You make it."

"You make it!" said Horrid Henry.

"You make it!" said Bossy Bill.

132

"No," said Henry.

"Yes," said Bill. "It's my dad's company and you have to do what I say."

"No I don't!" said Henry.

"Yes you do," said Bill.

"I don't work for you," said Henry.

"Yeah, but your dad works for *my* dad," said Bossy Bill. "If you don't do what I say I'll tell my dad to fire your dad."

Horrid Henry glared at Bossy Bill, then slowly switched on the kettle. When he was king he'd build a shark tank specially for Bill.

Bossy Bill folded his arms and smirked as Henry poured hot water over the teabags. What a creep, thought Henry, licking his fingers and dipping them into the sugar bowl.

"You're disgusting," said Bossy Bill. "I'm telling on you."

"Go ahead," said Henry, licking sugar off his fingers. Next to his cousin Stuck-up Steve, Bossy Bill was the yuckiest kid he had ever met.

"Hey, I've got a great idea," said Bill. "Let's put salt in the tea instead of sugar."

Horrid Henry hesitated. But hadn't Dad said to do what Bill told him?

"Okay," said Henry.

Bossy Bill poured a heaped teaspoon of salt into every cup.

"Now watch this," said Bill.

"Thank you, Bill," said Mr String. "Aren't you clever!"

"Thank you, Bill," said Ms Bean.

134

"Aren't you wonderful!"

"Thanks, Bill," said Big Boss. "How's the tea, everyone?"

"Delicious," said Mr String. He put down the cup.

"Delightful," said Ms Bean. She put down the cup.

"Umm," said Dad. He put down the cup.

Then Big Boss took a sip. His face curdled.

"Disgusting!" he gasped, spitting out the tea. "Bleeeach! Who put salt in this?"

"Henry did," said Bill.

Horrid Henry was outraged.

"Liar!" said Henry. "You did!"

"This tea is revolting," said Mr String.

"Horrible," said Ms Bean.

"I tried to stop him, Dad, but he just wouldn't listen," said Bossy Bill.

"I'm disappointed in you, Henry," said Big Boss. "Bill would never do anything like this." He glanced at Dad. Dad looked as if he wished an alien  spaceship would beam him up.

"But I didn't do it!" said Henry. He stared at Bill. What a creep!

"Now run along boys, and help answer the phones. Bill will show you how, Henry," said Big Boss.

Horrid Henry followed Bill out of the meeting room. Beware, Bill, he thought. I'll get you for this.

136

Bill sat down at a huge desk and swung his feet up.

"Now copy me," he said. "Answer the phones just like I do."

Ring ring.

"Hello, Elephant House!" said Bill.

Ring ring.

"Hello! Tootsie's Take-Away!" said Bill.

Ring ring.

"Hello! Pizza Parlour!" said Bill.

Ring ring.

"Go on, Henry, answer it."

"No!" said Henry. After what had just

happened with the tea, he'd never trust Bill again.

Ring ring.

"What are you, chicken?" said Bill.

"No," said Henry.

"Then go on. *I* did it."

Ring ring ring ring.

"All right," said Henry. He picked up the phone. He'd just do it once.

"Hello Smelly! You're fired!"

Silence.

"Is that you, Henry?" said Big Boss on the other end of the phone.

Eeek!

"Wrong number!" squeaked Horrid Henry, and slammed down the phone. Uh oh. Now he was in trouble. Big big trouble.

Big Boss stormed
into the room.

"What's going on in
here?"

"I tried to stop him,
but he just wouldn't
listen," said Bossy Bill.

"That's not true!" squealed Horrid
Henry. "You started it."

"As if," said Bossy Bill.

"And what have you been doing, son?"
asked Big Boss.

"Testing the phones for you," said
Bossy Bill. "I think there's a fault on line
2. I'll fix it in a minute."

"That's my little genius," beamed Big
Boss. He glared at Henry. Henry glared
back.

"I told you to follow Bill's example!"
hissed Dad.

"I did!" hissed Henry.

Bossy Bill and Big Boss exchanged pitying glances.

"He's not usually like this," lied Dad. He looked as if he wished a whirlwind would whisk him away.

"I am usually like this!" said Henry. "Just not today!"

"No pocket money for a year if there's any more trouble," muttered Dad.

This was so unfair. Why should he get blamed when it was absolutely definitely not his fault?

"I'll give you one more chance," said Big Boss. He handed Henry a stack of papers. "Photocopy these for the meeting this afternoon," he said. "If there are any more problems I will ask your father to take you home."

Take him home! Dad would never ever forgive him. He was mad enough at Henry already. And it was all Bill's fault.

Scowling, Horrid Henry followed Bill
into the photocopy room.

"Ha ha ha ha ha, I got you into
trouble!" chortled Bill.

Horrid Henry resisted the urge to
mash Bossy Bill into tiny bite-sized
chunks. Instead, Horrid Henry started to
think. Even if he was good as gold all day

it would mean Bill had won. He had to come up with a plan to get back at Bill. Fast. But what? Anything awful Bill did Henry was sure to get the blame. No one would believe Henry hadn't done it. If his plan was to work, Bill had to be caught red-handed.

And then Horrid Henry had it. A perfectly brilliant, spectacularly evil plan. A plan to end all plans. A plan to go down in history. A plan – but there was no time to lose congratulating himself.

Bossy Bill snatched the papers from Henry's hand.

"I get to do the photocopying because it's *my* dad's office," he said. "If you're good I might let you hand out the papers."

"Whatever you say," said Horrid Henry humbly. "After all, you're the boss."

"Too right I am," said Bossy Bill.
"Everyone has to do what I say."

"Of course," said Horrid Henry
agreeably. "Hey, I've got a great idea," he
added after a moment, "why don't we
make horrid faces, photocopy them and
hang the pictures all round the meeting
room?"

Bossy Bill's eyes gleamed. "Yeah!" he
said. He stuck out his tongue. He made a
monkey face. He twisted his lips. "Heh
heh heh." Then he paused. "Wait a
minute. We'd be recognised."

Aaargh! Horrid Henry hadn't thought
of that. His beautiful plan crumpled

before him. Bill would win. Henry would lose. The terrible image of Bossy Bill laughing at him from here to eternity loomed before him. NO! No one ever tricked Horrid Henry and lived. I need a change of plan, thought Henry desperately. And then he knew what had to be done. It was risky. It was dangerous. But it was the only way.

"I know," said Horrid Henry. "Let's photocopy our bottoms instead."

"Yeah!" said Bossy Bill. "I was just going to suggest that."

"I get to go first," said Horrid Henry, shoving Bill out of the way.

"No, I do!" said Bill, shoving him back. YES! thought Horrid Henry, as Bill hopped onto the photocopier. "*You* can paste up the pictures in the meeting room."

"Great!" said Henry. He could tell

what Bill was thinking. He'd get his dad to come in while Henry was sellotaping pictures of bottoms around the meeting room.

"I'll just get the sellotape," said Henry.

"You do that," said Bossy Bill, as the photocopier whirred into life.

Horrid Henry ran down the hall into Big Boss's office.

"Come quick, Bill's in trouble!" said Horrid Henry.

Big Boss dropped the phone and raced down the hall after Henry.

"Hold on, Bill, Daddy's coming!" he shrieked, and burst into the photocopy room.

There was Bossy Bill, perched on the photocopier, his back to the door, singing merrily:

"One bottom, two bottoms, three bottoms, four,

Five bottoms, six bottoms, seven bottoms, more!"

"Bill!" screamed Big Boss.

"It was Henry!" screamed Bossy Bill. "I was just testing the photocopier to make sure—"

"Be quiet, Bill!" shouted Big Boss. "I saw what you were doing."

"I tried to stop him but he just wouldn't listen," said Horrid Henry.

Horrid Henry spent a lovely rest of the day at Dad's office. After Bill was grounded for a month and sent home in disgrace, Henry twirled all the chairs round and round. He sneaked up behind people and shouted, "Boo!" Then he ate doughnuts, played computer games, and surfed the web. Boy, working in an office is fun, thought Horrid Henry. I'm going to enjoy getting a job when I grow up.

4

··

HORRID HENRY
AND THE
DEMON DINNER LADY

"You're not having a packed lunch and
that's final," yelled Dad.

"It's not fair!" yelled Horrid Henry.
"Everyone in my class has a packed lunch."

"N-O spells no," said Dad. "It's too
much work. And you never eat what I
pack for you."

"But I hate school dinners!" screamed
Henry. "I'm being poisoned!" He
clutched his throat. "Dessert today was—
bleeeach—fruit salad! And it had worms in
it! I can feel them slithering in my stomach

– uggghh!" Horrid Henry fell to the floor, gasping and rasping.

Mum continued watching TV.

Dad continued watching TV.

"I love school dinners," said Perfect Peter. "They're so nutritious and delicious. Especially those lovely spinach salads."

"Shut up, Peter!" snarled Henry.

"Muuuum!" wailed Peter. "Henry told me to shut up!"

"Don't be horrid, Henry!" said Mum. "You're not having a packed lunch and that's that."

Horrid Henry and his parents had been fighting about packed lunches for weeks. Henry was desperate to have a packed lunch. Actually, he was desperate *not* to have a school dinner.

Horrid Henry hated school dinners. The stinky smell. The terrible way Sloppy Sally ladled the food *splat!* on his tray so that most of it splashed all over him. And the food! Queueing for hours for revolting ravioli and squashed tomatoes. The lumpy custard. The blobby mashed potatoes. Horrid Henry could not bear it any longer.

151

"Oh please," said Henry. "I'll make the packed lunch myself." Wouldn't that be great! He'd fill his lunchbox with four packs of crisps, chocolate, doughnuts, cake, lollies, and one grape. Now that's what I call a real lunch, thought Henry.

Mum sighed.

Dad sighed.

They looked at each other.

"If you promise that everything in your lunchbox will get eaten, then I'll do a packed lunch for you," said Dad.

"Oh thank you thank you thank you!" said Horrid Henry. "Everything will get eaten, I promise." Just not by me, he thought gleefully. Packed lunch room, here I come. Food fights, food swaps, food fun at last. Yippee!

Horrid Henry strolled into the packed lunch room. He was King Henry the

152

Horrible, surveying his unruly subjects.
All around him children were screaming
and shouting, pushing and shoving,
throwing food and trading treats. Heaven!
Horrid Henry smiled happily and opened
his Mutant Max lunchbox.

Hmmn. An egg salad sandwich. On
brown bread. With crusts. Yuck! But he
could always swap it for one of Greedy
Graham's stack of chocolate spread
sandwiches. Or one of Rude Ralph's jam

rolls. That was the great thing about packed lunches, thought Henry. Someone always wanted what you had. No one *ever* wanted someone else's school dinner. Henry shuddered.

But those bad days were behind him, part of the dim and distant past. A horror story to tell his grandchildren. Henry could see it now. A row of horrified toddlers, screaming and crying while he told terrifying tales of stringy stew and soggy semolina.

Now, what else? Henry's fingers closed on something round. An apple. Great, thought Henry, he could use it for target practice, and the carrots would be perfect for poking Gorgeous Gurinder when she wasn't looking.

Henry dug deeper. What was buried right at the bottom? What was hidden under the celery sticks and the granola bar? Oh boy! Crisps! Henry loved crisps. So salty! So crunchy! So yummy! His mean, horrible parents only let him have crisps once a week. Crisps! What bliss! He could taste their delicious saltiness already. He wouldn't share them with anyone, no matter how hard they begged. Henry tore open the bag and reached in—

Suddenly a huge shadow fell over him. A fat greasy hand shot out. Snatch! Crunch. Crunch.

Horrid Henry's crisps were gone.

Henry was so shocked that for a moment he could not speak. "Wha—wha—what was that?" gasped Henry as a gigantic woman waddled between the tables. "She just stole my crisps!"

"That," said Rude Ralph grimly, "was Greta. She's the demon dinner lady."

"Watch out for her!" squealed Sour Susan.

"She's the sneakiest snatcher in school," wailed Weepy William.

What? A dinner lady who snatched food instead of dumping it on your plate? How could this be? Henry stared as Greasy Greta patrolled up and down the aisles. Her piggy eyes darted from side to side. She ignored Aerobic Al's carrots. She ignored Tidy Ted's yoghurt. She ignored Goody-Goody Gordon's orange.

Then suddenly—

Snatch! Chomp. Chomp.
Sour Susan's sweets were gone.
Snatch! Chomp. Chomp.
Dizzy Dave's doughnut was
gone.

Snatch! Chomp.
Chomp. Beefy Bert's
biscuits were gone.
Moody Margaret
looked up from her
lunch.

"Don't look up!" shrieked Susan. Too
late! Greasy Greta swept Margaret's food
away, stuffing Margaret's uneaten
chocolate bar into her fat wobbly cheeks.

"Hey, I wasn't finished!" screamed
Margaret. Greasy Greta ignored her and
marched on. Weepy William tried to hide
his toffees under his cheese sandwich. But
Greasy Greta wasn't fooled.

Snatch! Gobble. Gobble. The toffees

vanished down Greta's gaping gob.

"Waaah," wailed William. "I want my toffees!"

"No sweets in school," barked Greasy Greta. She marched up and down, up and down, snatching and grabbing, looting and devouring, wobbling and gobbling.

Why had no one told him there was a demon dinner lady in charge of the packed lunch room?

"Why didn't you warn me about her, Ralph?" demanded Henry.

Rude Ralph shrugged. "It wouldn't have done any good. She is unstoppable."

We'll see about that, thought Henry. He glared at Greta. No way would Greasy Greta grab his food again.

On Tuesday Greta snatched Henry's doughnut.

On Wednesday Greta snatched Henry's cake.

On Thursday Greta snatched Henry's biscuits.

On Friday, as usual, Horrid Henry
persuaded Anxious Andrew to swap his
crisps for Henry's granola bar. He
persuaded Kung-Fu Kate to swap her
chocolates for Henry's raisins. He
persuaded Beefy Bert to swap his biscuits
for Henry's carrots. But what was the use
of being a brilliant food trader, thought
Henry miserably, if Greasy Greta just
swooped and snaffled his hard-won treats?

Henry tried hiding his desserts. He
tried eating his desserts secretly. He tried
tugging them back. But it was no use.

The moment he snapped open his lunch box – SNATCH! Greasy Greta grabbed the goodies.

Something had to be done.

"Mum," complained Henry, "there's a demon dinner lady at school snatching our sweets."

"That's nice, Henry," said Mum, reading her newspaper.

"Dad," complained Henry, "there's a demon dinner lady at school snatching our sweets."

"Good," said Dad. "You eat too many sweets."

"We're not allowed to bring sweets to school, Henry," said Perfect Peter.

"But it's not fair!" squealed Henry. "She takes crisps, too."

"If you don't like it, go back to school dinners," said Dad.

"No!" howled Henry. "I hate school dinners!" Watery gravy with bits. Lumpy surprise with lumps. Gristly glop with

globules. Food with its own life slopping about on his tray. NO! Horrid Henry couldn't face it. He'd fought so hard for a packed lunch. Even a packed lunch like the one Dad made, fortified with eight essential minerals and vitamins, was better than going back to school dinners.

He could, of course, just eat healthy foods. Greta never snatched those. Henry imagined his lunchbox, groaning with alfalfa sprouts on wholemeal brown bread studded with chewy bits. Ugh! Bleeeach! Torture!

He had to keep his packed lunch. But he had to stop Greta. He just had to.

And then suddenly Henry had a brilliant, spectacular idea. It was so brilliant that for a moment he could hardly believe he'd thought of it. Oh boy, Greta, thought Henry gleefully, are you going to be sorry you messed with me.

Lunchtime. Horrid Henry sat with his lunchbox unopened. Rude Ralph was armed and ready beside him. Now, where was Greta?

Thump. Thump. Thump. The floor shook as the demon dinner lady started her food patrol. Horrid Henry waited

163

until she was almost behind him. SNAP!
He opened his lunchbox.

SNATCH! The familiar greasy hand
shot out, grabbed Henry's biscuits and
shovelled them into her mouth. Her
terrible teeth began to chomp.

And then—-

"Yiaowwww! Aaaarrrgh!" A terrible
scream echoed through the packed lunch
room.

Greasy Greta turned purple. Then pink. Then bright red.

"Yiaowwww!" she howled. "I need to cool down! Gimme that!" she screeched, snatching Rude Ralph's doughnut and stuffing it in her mouth.

"Aaaarrrgh!" she choked. "I'm on fire! Water! Water!"

She grabbed a pitcher of water, poured it on top of herself, then ran howling down the aisle and out the door.

For a moment there was silence. Then the entire packed lunch room started clapping and cheering.

"Wow, Henry," said Greedy Graham, "What did you do to her?"

"Nothing," said Horrid Henry. "She just tried my special recipe. Hot chilli powder biscuits, anyone?"

HORRID
HENRY
AND THE
BOGEY BABYSITTER

*To my old friends Caroline Elton and
Andrew Franklin, and my new ones
Miriam, Jonathan, and Michael*

CONTENTS

1

HORRID HENRY
TRICKS AND TREATS

Hallowe'en! Oh happy, happy day!
Every year Horrid Henry could not
believe it: an entire day devoted to
stuffing your face with sweets and
playing horrid tricks. Best of all, you
were *supposed* to stuff your face and
play horrid tricks. Whoopee!

Horrid Henry was armed and ready.
He had loo roll. He had water pistols.
He had shaving foam. Oh my, would he
be playing tricks tonight. Anyone who
didn't instantly hand over a fistful of
sweets would get it with the foam. And
woe betide any fool who gave him an
apple. Horrid Henry knew how to treat

rotten grown-ups like that.

His red and black devil costume lay ready on the bed, complete with evil mask, twinkling horns, trident, and whippy tail. He'd scare everyone wearing that.

"Heh heh heh," said Horrid Henry, practising his evil laugh.

"Henry," came a little voice outside his bedroom door, "come and see my new costume."

"No," said Henry.

"Oh please, Henry," said his younger brother, Perfect Peter.

"No," said Henry. "I'm busy."

"You're just jealous because *my* costume is nicer than yours," said Peter.

"Am not."

"Are too."

Come to think of it, what *was* Peter wearing? Last year he'd copied Henry's monster costume and ruined Henry's Hallowe'en. What if he were copying

Henry's devil costume? That would be just like that horrible little copycat.

"All right, you can come in for two seconds," said Henry.

A big, pink bouncy bunny bounded into Henry's room. It had little white bunny ears. It had a little white bunny tail. It had pink polka dots everywhere else. Horrid Henry groaned. What a stupid costume. Thank goodness *he* wasn't wearing it.

"Isn't it great?" said Perfect Peter.

"No," said Henry. "It's horrible."

"You're just saying that to be mean, Henry," said Peter, bouncing up and down. "I can't wait to go trick-or-treating in it tonight."

Oh no. Horrid Henry felt as if he'd been punched in the stomach. Henry would be expected to go out trick or treating – with Peter! He, Henry, would have to walk around with a pink polka dot bunny. Everyone would see him. The shame of it! Rude Ralph would never stop teasing him. Moody Margaret would call him a bunny wunny. How could he play tricks on people with a pink polka dot bunny following him everywhere? He was ruined. His name would be a joke.

"You can't wear that," said Henry desperately.

"Yes I can," said Peter.

"I won't let you," said Henry.

Perfect Peter looked at Henry. "You're just jealous."

Grrr! Horrid Henry was about to tear that stupid costume off Peter when, suddenly, he had an idea.

It was painful.

It was humiliating.

But anything was better than having Peter prancing about in pink polka dots.

"Tell you what," said Henry, "just because I'm so nice I'll let you borrow my monster costume. You've always wanted to wear it."

"NO!" said Peter. "I want to be a bunny."

"But you're supposed to be scary for Hallowe'en," said Henry.

"I am scary," said Peter. "I'm going to bounce up to people and yell 'boo'."

"I can make you really scary, Peter," said Horrid Henry.

"How?" said Peter.

"Sit down and I'll show you." Henry patted his desk chair.

"What are you going to do?" said Peter suspiciously. He took a step back.

"Nothing," said Henry. "I'm just trying to help you."

Perfect Peter didn't move.

"How can I be scarier?" he said cautiously.

"I can give you a scary haircut," said Henry.

Perfect Peter clutched his curls.

"But I like my hair," he said feebly.

176

"This is Hallowe'en," said
Henry. "Do you want to
be scary or don't you?"

"Um, um, uh," said
Peter, as Henry pushed
him down in the chair and
got out the scissors.

"Not too much," squealed Peter.

"Of course not," said Horrid Henry.
"Just sit back and relax, I promise you'll
love this."

Horrid Henry twirled the scissors.
Snip! Snip! Snip! Snip! Snip!

Magnificent, thought Horrid Henry.
He gazed proudly at his work. Maybe he
should be a hairdresser when he grew up.
Yes! Henry could see it now. Customers
would queue for miles for one of
Monsieur Henri's scary snips. Shame his
genius was wasted on someone as yucky
as Peter. Still…

"You look great, Peter," said Henry. "Really scary. Atomic Bunny. Go and have a look."

Peter went over and looked in the mirror.

"AAAAAAAAAARGGGGGGG!"

"Scared yourself, did you?" said Henry. "That's great."

"AAAAAAAAAARGGGGGGG!" howled Peter.

Mum ran into the room.

"AAAAAAAAAARGGGGGGG!" howled Mum.

"AAAAAAAAAARGGGGGGG!" howled Peter.

"Henry!" screeched Mum. "What have you done! You horrid, horrid boy!"

 What was left of Peter's hair stuck up in ragged tufts all over his head. On one side was a big bald patch.

"I was just making

178

him look scary,"
protested Henry. "He
said I could."

"Henry made me!"
said Peter.

"My poor baby," said
Mum. She glared at Henry.

"No trick-or-treating for you," said
Mum. "You'll stay here."

Horrid Henry could hardly believe his
ears. This was the worst thing that had
ever happened to him.

"NO!" howled Henry. This was all
Peter's fault.

"I hate you Peter!" he screeched. Then
he attacked. He was Medusa, coiling
round her victim with her snaky hair.

"Aaaahh!" screeched Peter.

"Henry!" shouted Mum. "Go to your
room!"

★

Mum and Peter left the house to go
trick-or-treating. Henry had screamed
and sobbed and begged. He'd put on
his devil costume, just in case his tears
melted their stony hearts. But no. His
mean, horrible parents wouldn't change
their mind. Well, they'd be sorry.
They'd all be sorry.

Dad came into the sitting room. He
was holding a large shopping bag.

"Henry, I've got some work to finish so
I'm going to let you hand out treats to
any trick-or-treaters."

Horrid Henry stopped plotting his
revenge. Had Dad gone mad? Hand out
treats? What kind of
punishment was this?

Horrid Henry
fought to keep a big
smile off his face.

"Here's the
Hallowe'en stuff,

180

Henry," said Dad. He handed Henry the
heavy bag. "But remember," he added
sternly, "these treats are not for you:
they're to give away."

Yeah, right, thought Henry.

"OK Dad," he said as meekly as he
could. "Whatever you say."

Dad went back to the kitchen. Now
was his chance! Horrid Henry leapt on
the bag. Wow, was it full! He'd grab all
the good stuff, throw back anything
yucky with lime or peppermint, and he'd
have enough sweets to keep him going
for at least a week!

Henry yanked open the bag. A terrible
sight met his eyes. The bag was full of

satsumas. And apples. And walnuts in
their shells. No wonder his horrible
parents had trusted him to be in charge
of it.

Ding dong.

Slowly, Horrid Henry heaved his heavy
bones to the door. There was his empty,
useless trick-or-treat bag, sitting forlornly
by the entrance. Henry gave it a kick,
then opened the door and glared.

"Whaddya want?"
snapped Horrid Henry.

"Trick-or-treat," whis-
pered Weepy William.
He was dressed as a
pirate.

Horrid Henry held
out the bag of horrors.

"Lucky dip!" he
announced. "Close
your eyes for a big
surprise!"

182

William certainly would
be surprised at what a
rotten treat he'd be
getting.

Weepy William put
down his swag bag, closed
his eyes tight, then plunged his hand into
Henry's lucky dip. He rummaged and he
rummaged and he rummaged, hoping to
find something better than satsumas.

Horrid Henry eyed Weepy William's
bulging swag bag.

Go on Henry, urged the bag. He'll
never notice.

Horrid Henry did not wait to be asked
twice.

Dip!

Zip!

Pop!

Horrid Henry grabbed a big handful of
William's sweets and popped them inside
his empty bag.

Weepy William opened his eyes.

"Did you take some of my sweets?"

"No," said Henry.

William peeked inside his bag and burst into tears.

"Waaaaaaaa!" wailed William. "Henry took – "

Henry pushed him out and slammed the door.

Dad came running.

"What's wrong?"

"Nothing," said Henry. "Just William crying 'cause he's scared of pumpkins."

Phew, thought Henry. That was close. Perhaps he had been a little too greedy.

Ding dong. It was Lazy Linda wearing a pillowcase over her head. Gorgeous Gurinder was with her, dressed as a scarecrow.

"Trick-or-treat!"

"Trick-or-treat!"

"Close your eyes for a big surprise!" said Henry, holding out the lucky dip bag.

"Ooh, a lucky dip!" squealed Linda.

Lazy Linda and Gorgeous Gurinder put down their bags, closed their eyes, and reached into the lucky dip.

Dip!

Zip!

Pop!

Dip!

Zip!

Pop!

Lazy Linda opened her eyes.

"You give the worst treats ever, Henry," said Linda, gazing at her walnut in disgust.

"We won't be coming back *here*,"

sniffed Gorgeous Gurinder.

Tee hee, thought Horrid Henry.

Ding dong.

It was Beefy Bert. He was wearing a robot costume.

"Hi Bert, got any good sweets?" asked Henry.

"I dunno," said Beefy Bert.

Horrid Henry soon found out that he did. Lots and lots and lots of them. So did Moody Margaret, Sour Susan, Jolly Josh and Tidy Ted. Soon Henry's bag was stuffed with treats.

Ding dong.

Horrid Henry opened the door.

"Boo," said Atomic Bunny.

Henry's sweet bag! Help! Mum would see it!

"Eeeeek!" screeched Horrid Henry. "Help! Save me!"

Quickly, he ran upstairs clutching his bag and hid it safely under his bed. Phew, that was close.

"Don't be scared, Henry, it's only me," called Perfect Peter.

Horrid Henry came back downstairs.

"No!" said Henry. "I'd never have known."

"Really?" said Peter.

"Really," said Henry.

"Everyone just gave sweets this year," said Perfect Peter. "Yuck."

Horrid Henry held out the lucky dip.

"Ooh, a satsuma," said Peter. "Aren't I lucky!"

"I hope you've learned your lesson, Henry," said Mum sternly.

"I certainly have," said Horrid Henry, eyeing Perfect Peter's bulging bag. "Good things come to those who wait."

2

HORRID HENRY
AND THE
BOGEY BABYSITTER

"No way!" shrieked Tetchy Tess,
slamming down the phone.

"No way!" shrieked Crabby Chris,
slamming down the phone.

"No way!" shrieked Angry Anna.
"What do you think I am, crazy?"

Even Mellow Martin said he was busy.

Mum hung up the phone and groaned.

It wasn't easy finding someone to
babysit more than once for Horrid
Henry. When Tetchy Tess came, Henry
flooded the bathroom. When Crabby
Chris came he hid her homework and

"accidentally" poured red grape juice down the front of her new white jeans. And when Angry Anna came Henry – no, it's too dreadful. Suffice it to say that Anna ran screaming from the house and Henry's parents had to come home early.

Horrid Henry hated babysitters. He wasn't a baby. He didn't want to be sat on. Why should he be nice to some ugly, stuck-up, bossy teenager who'd hog the TV and pig out on Henry's biscuits? Parents should just stay at home where they belonged, thought Horrid Henry.

And now it looked like they would have to. Ha! His parents were mean and horrible, but he'd had a lot of practice managing them. Babysitters were unpredictable. Babysitters were hard work. And by the time you'd broken them in and shown them who was boss, for some reason they didn't want to come any more. The only good babysitters let you

stay up all night and eat sweets until you
were sick. Sadly, Horrid Henry never got
one of those.

"We have to find a babysitter," wailed
Mum. "The party is tomorrow night.
I've tried everyone. Who else is there?"

"There's got to be someone," said Dad.
"Think!"

Mum thought.

Dad thought.

"What about Rebecca?" said Dad.

Horrid Henry's heart missed a beat.
He stopped drawing moustaches on
Perfect Peter's school pictures. Maybe

he'd heard wrong. Oh please, not Rebecca! Not – Rabid Rebecca!

"Who did you say?" asked Henry. His voice quavered.

"You heard me," said Dad. "Rebecca."

"NO!" screamed Henry. "She's horrible!"

"She's not horrible," said Dad. "She's just – strict."

"There's no one else," said Mum grimly. "I'll phone Rebecca."

"She's a monster!" wailed Henry. "She made Ralph go to bed at six o'clock!"

"I like going to bed at six o'clock," said Perfect Peter. "After all, growing children need their rest."

Horrid Henry growled and attacked. He was the Creature from the Black

Lagoon, dragging the foolish mortal down to a watery grave.

"AAAEEEEE!" squealed Peter. "Henry pulled my hair."

"Stop being horrid, Henry!" said Dad. "Mum's on the phone."

Henry prayed. Maybe she'd be busy. Maybe she'd say no. Maybe she'd be dead. He'd heard all about Rebecca. She'd made Tough Toby get in his pyjamas at five o'clock *and* do all his homework. She'd unplugged Dizzy Dave's computer.

She'd made Moody Margaret wash the
floor. No doubt about it, Rabid Rebecca
was the toughest teen in town.

Henry lay on the rug and howled.
Mum shouted into the phone.

"You can! That's great, Rebecca. No,
that's just the TV – sorry for the noise.
See you tomorrow."

"NOOOOOOOOO!" wailed Henry.

Ding dong.

"I'll get it!" said Perfect Peter. He
skipped to the door.

Henry flung himself on the carpet.

"I DON'T WANT TO HAVE A
BABYSITTER!" he wailed.

The door opened. In walked the
biggest, meanest, ugliest, nastiest-looking
girl Henry had ever seen. Her arms were
enormous. Her head was enormous.
Her teeth were enormous. She looked
like she ate elephants for breakfasts,

 crocodiles for lunch, and snacked on toddlers for tea.

"What have you got to eat?" snarled Rabid Rebecca.

Dad took a step back. "Help yourself to anything in the fridge," said Dad.

"Don't worry, I will," said Rebecca.

"GO HOME, YOU WITCH!" howled Henry.

"Bedtime is nine o'clock," shouted Dad, trying to be heard above Henry's screams. He edged his way carefully past Rebecca, jumped over Henry, then dashed out the front door.

"I DON'T WANT TO HAVE A BABYSITTER!" shrieked Henry.

"Be good, Henry," said Mum weakly. She stepped over Henry, then escaped from the house.

The door closed.

Horrid Henry was alone in the house with Rabid Rebecca.

He glared at Rebecca.

Rebecca glared at him.

"I've heard all about you, you little creep," growled Rebecca. "No one bothers me when I'm babysitting."

Horrid Henry stopped screaming.

"Oh yeah," said Horrid Henry. "We'll see about that."

Rabid Rebecca bared her fangs. Henry recoiled. Perhaps I'd better keep out of her way, he thought, then slipped into the sitting room and turned on the telly.

Ahh, Mutant Max. Hurray! How bad could life be when a brilliant program like Mutant Max was on? He'd annoy Rebecca as soon as it was over.

Rebecca stomped into the room and snatched the clicker.

ZAP!

DA DOO, DA DOO DA, DA DOO DA DOO DA, tangoed some horrible spangly dancers.

"Hey," said Henry. "I'm watching Mutant Max."

"Tough," said Rebecca. "*I'm* watching ballroom dancing."

Snatch!

Horrid Henry grabbed the clicker.

ZAP!

"And it's mutants, mutants, mut – "

Snatch!

Zap!

DA DOO, DA DOO DA, DA DOO
DA DOO DA.

DOO, DA DOO DA, DA DOO DA
DOO DA.

Horrid Henry tangoed round the
room, gliding and sliding.

"Stop it," muttered Rebecca.

Henry shimmied back and forth in
front of the telly, blocking her view and
singing along as loudly as he could.

"DA DOO, DA DOO DA," warbled
Henry.

"I'm warning you," hissed Rebecca.

Perfect Peter walked in. He had
already put on his blue bunny pyjamas,
brushed his teeth and combed his hair.
He held a game of Chinese Checkers in
his hand.

"Rebecca, will you play a game with
me before I go to bed?" asked Peter.

"NO!" roared Rebecca. "I'm trying to
watch TV. Shut up and go away."

Perfect Peter leapt back.

"But I thought – since I was all ready for bed – " he stammered.

"I've got better things to do than to play with you," snarled Rebecca. "Now go to bed this minute, both of you."

"But it's not my bedtime for hours," protested Henry. "I want to watch Mutant Max."

"Nor mine," said Perfect Peter timidly. "There's this nature programme – "

"GO!" howled Rebecca.

"NO!" howled Henry.

"RAAAAA!" roared Rabid Rebecca.

Horrid Henry did not know how it happened. It was as if fiery dragon's breath had blasted him upstairs. Somehow, he was in his pyjamas, in bed, and it was only seven o'clock.

Rabid Rebecca switched off the light. "Don't even think of moving from that bed," she hissed. "If I see you, or hear you, or even smell you, you'll be sorry you were born. I'll stay downstairs, you stay upstairs, and that way no one will get hurt." Then she marched out of the room and slammed the door.

Horrid Henry was so shocked he could not move. He, Horrid Henry, the bull-dozer of babysitters, the terror of teach-ers, the bully of brothers, was in bed, lights out, at seven o'clock.

Seven o'clock! Two whole hours before his bedtime! This was an outrage! He could hear Moody Margaret shrieking next door. He could hear Toddler Tom zooming about on his tricycle. No one went to bed at seven o'clock. Not even toddlers!

Worst of all, he was thirsty. So what if she told me to stay in bed, thought Horrid Henry. I'm thirsty. I'm going to go downstairs and get myself a glass of water. It's my house and I'll do what I want.

Horrid Henry did not move.

I'm dying of thirst here, thought Henry. Mum and Dad will come home and I'll

be a dried out old stick insect, and boy will she be in trouble.

Horrid Henry still did not move.

Go on, feet, urged Henry, let's just step on down and get a little ol' glass of water. So what if that bogey babysitter said he had to stay in bed. What could she do to him?

She could chop off my head and bounce it down the stairs, thought Henry.

Eeek.

Well, let her try.

Horrid Henry remembered who he was. The boy who'd sent teachers shrieking from the classroom. The boy who'd destroyed the Demon Dinner Lady. The boy who had run away from home and almost reached the Congo.

I will get up and get a drink of water, he thought.

Sneak. Sneak. Sneak.

Horrid Henry crept to the bedroom door.

Slowly he opened it a crack.

Creak.

Then slowly, slowly, he opened the door a bit more and slipped out.

ARGHHHHHH!

There was Rabid Rebecca sitting at the top of the stairs.

It's a trap, thought Henry. She was lying in wait for me. I'm dead, I'm finished, they'll find my bones in the morning.

Horrid Henry dashed back inside his room and awaited his doom.

Silence.

What was going on? Why hadn't Rebecca torn him apart limb from limb?

Horrid Henry opened his door a fraction and peeped out.

Rabid Rebecca was still sitting huddled at the top of the stairs. She did not move. Her eyes were fixed straight ahead.

"Spi–spi–spider," she whispered. She pointed at a big, hairy spider in front of her with a trembling hand.

"It's huge," said Henry. "Really hairy and horrible and wriggly and – "

"STOP!" squealed Rebecca. "Help me, Henry," she begged.

Horrid Henry was not the fearless leader of a pirate gang for nothing.

"If I risk my life and get rid of the spider, can I watch Mutant Max?" said Henry.

"Yes," said Rebecca.

"And stay up 'til my parents come home?"

"Yes," said Rebecca.

"And eat all the ice cream in the fridge?"

"YES!" shrieked Rebecca. "Just get rid of that — that — "

"Deal," said Horrid Henry.

He dashed to his room and grabbed a jar.

Rabid Rebecca hid her eyes as Horrid Henry scooped up the spider. What a beauty!

"It's gone," said Henry.

Rebecca opened her beady red eyes.

"Right, back to bed, you little brat!"

"What?" said Henry.

"Bed. Now!" screeched Rebecca.

"But we agreed…" said Henry.

"Tough," said Rebecca. "That was then."

"Traitor," said Henry.

He whipped out the spider jar from behind his back and unscrewed the lid.

"On guard!" he said.

"AAEEEE!" whimpered Rebecca.

Horrid Henry advanced menacingly towards her.

"NOOOOOOO!" wailed Rebecca, stepping back.

"Now get in that room and stay there," ordered Henry. "Or else."

Rabid Rebecca skedaddled into the bathroom and locked the door.

"If I see you or hear you or even smell you you'll be sorry you were born," said Henry.

"I already am," said
Rabid Rebecca.

Horrid Henry spent
a lovely evening in
front of the telly. He
watched scary movies.
He ate ice cream and sweets and biscuits
and crisps until he could stuff no more
in.

Vroom vroom.

Oops. Parents home.

Horrid Henry dashed upstairs and leapt
into bed just as the front door opened.

Mum and Dad looked around the sitting room, littered with sweet wrappers,
biscuit crumbs and ice cream cartons.

"You did tell her to help herself," said
Mum.

"Still," said Dad. "What a pig."

"Never mind," said Mum brightly, "at
least she managed to get Henry to bed.

That's a first."

Rabid Rebecca staggered into the room.

"Did you get enough to eat?" said Dad.

"No," said Rabid Rebecca.

"Oh," said Dad.

"Was everything all right?" asked Mum.

Rebecca looked at her.

"Can I go now?" said Rebecca.

"Any chance you could babysit on

214

Saturday?" asked Dad hopefully.

"What do you think I am, crazy?" shrieked Rebecca.

SLAM!

Upstairs, Horrid Henry groaned.

Rats. It was so unfair. Just when he had a babysitter beautifully trained, for some reason they wouldn't come back.

3

HORRID HENRY'S RAID

"You're such a pig, Susan!"

"No I'm not! You're the pig!"

"You are!" squealed Moody Margaret.

"You are!" squealed Sour Susan.

"Oink!"

"Oink!"

All was not well at Moody Margaret's Secret Club.

Sour Susan and Moody Margaret glared at each other inside the Secret Club tent. Moody Margaret waved the empty biscuit tin in Susan's sour face.

"*Someone* ate all the biscuits," said Moody Margaret. "And it wasn't me."

"Well, it wasn't me," said Susan.

"Liar!"

"Liar!"

Margaret stuck out her tongue at Susan.

Susan stuck out her tongue at Margaret.

Margaret yanked Susan's hair.

"Oww! You horrible meanie!" shrieked Susan. "I hate you."

She yanked Margaret's hair.

"OWWW!" screeched Moody Margaret. "How dare you?"

They scowled at each other.

"Wait a minute," said Margaret. "You don't think – "

★

Not a million miles
away, sitting on a
throne inside the
Purple Hand fort
hidden behind
prickly branches,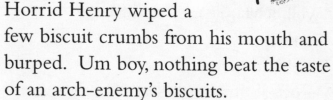
Horrid Henry wiped a
few biscuit crumbs from his mouth and
burped. Um boy, nothing beat the taste
of an arch-enemy's biscuits.

The branches parted.

"Password!" hissed Horrid Henry.

"Smelly toads."

"Enter," said Henry.

The sentry entered and gave the secret
handshake.

"Henry, why – " began Perfect Peter.

"Call me by my title, Worm!"

"Sorry, Henry – I mean Lord High
Excellent Majesty of the Purple Hand."

"That's better," said Henry. He waved
his hand and pointed at the ground. "Be

seated, Worm."

"Why am I Worm and you're Lord High Excellent Majesty?"

"Because I'm the Leader," said Henry.

"I want a better title," said Peter.

"All right," said the Lord High Excellent Majesty, "you can be Lord Worm."

Peter considered.

"What about Lord High Worm?"

"OK," said Henry. Then he froze.

"Worm! Footsteps!"

Perfect Peter peeked through the leaves.

"Enemies approaching!" he warned.

Pounding feet paused outside the entrance.

"Password!" said Horrid Henry.

"Dog poo breath," said Margaret, bursting in. Sour Susan followed.

"That's not the password," said Henry.

"You can't come in," squeaked the sentry, a little late.

"You've been stealing the Secret Club biscuits," said Moody Margaret.

"Yeah, Henry," said Susan.

Horrid Henry stretched and yawned.

"Prove it."

Moody Margaret pointed to all the crumbs lying on the dirt floor.

"Where did all these crumbs come from, then?"

"Biscuits," said Henry.

"So you admit it!" shrieked Margaret.

"Purple Hand biscuits," said Henry. He pointed to the Purple Hand skull and crossbones biscuit tin.

"Liar, liar, pants on fire," said Margaret.

Horrid Henry fell to the floor and started rolling around.

"Ooh, ooh, my pants are on fire, I'm burning, call the fire brigade!" shouted Henry.

Perfect Peter dashed off.

"Mum!" he hollered. "Henry's pants are on fire!"

Margaret and Susan made a hasty retreat.

Horrid Henry stopped rolling and howled with laughter.

"Ha ha ha ha ha – the Purple Hand rules!" he cackled.

"We'll get you for this, Henry," said Margaret.

"Yeah, yeah," said Henry.

"You didn't really steal their biscuits, did you Henry?" asked Lord High Worm the following day.

"As if," said Horrid Henry. "Now get back to your guard duty. Our enemies may be planning a revenge attack."

"Why do I always have to be the guard?" said Peter. "It's not fair."

"Whose club is this?" said Henry fiercely.

Peter's lip began to tremble.

"Yours," muttered Peter.

"So if you want to stay as a temporary member, you have to do what I say," said Henry.

"OK," said Peter.

"And remember, one day, if you're very good, you'll be promoted from junior sentry to chief sentry," said Henry.

"Ooh," said Peter, brightening.

Business settled, Horrid Henry reached for the biscuit tin. He'd saved five yummy chocolate fudge chewies for today.

Henry picked up the tin and stopped. Why wasn't it rattling? He shook it.

Silence.

Horrid Henry ripped off the lid and shrieked.

The Purple Hand biscuit tin was empty. Except for one thing. A dagger drawn on a piece of paper. The dastardly

mark of Margaret's Secret Club! Well, he'd show them who ruled.

"Worm!" he shrieked. "Get in here!"

Peter entered.

"We've been raided!" screamed Henry. "You're fired!"

"Waaaah!" wailed Peter.

"Good work, Susan," said the Leader of the Secret Club, her face covered in chocolate.

"I don't see why you got three biscuits and I only got two when I was the one who sneaked in and stole them," said Susan sourly.

"Tribute to your Leader," said Moody Margaret.

"I still don't think it's fair," muttered Susan.

"Tough," said Margaret. "Now let's hear your spy report."

"NAH NAH NEE NAH NAH!"

screeched a voice from outside.

Susan and Margaret dashed out of the Secret Club tent. They were too late. There was Henry, prancing off, waving the Secret Club banner he'd stolen.

"Give that back, Henry!" screamed Margaret.

"Make me!" said Henry.

Susan chased him. Henry darted.

Margaret chased him. Henry dodged.

"Come and get me!" taunted Henry.

"All right," said Margaret. She walked

towards him, then suddenly jumped over the wall into Henry's garden and ran to the Purple Hand fort.

"Hey, get away from there!" shouted Henry, chasing after her. Where was that useless sentry when you needed him?

Margaret nabbed Henry's skull and crossbones flag, and darted off.

The two Leaders faced each other.

"Gimme my flag!" ordered Henry.

"Gimme my flag!" ordered Margaret.

"You first," said Henry.

"*You* first," said Margaret.

Neither moved.

"OK, at the count of three we'll throw them to each other," said Margaret. One, two, three — throw!"

Margaret held on to Henry's flag.

Henry held on to Margaret's flag.

Several moments passed.

"Cheater," said Margaret.

"Cheater," said Henry.

"I don't know about you, but I have important spying work to get on with," said Margaret.

"So?" said Henry. "Get on with it. No one's stopping you."

"Drop my flag, Henry," said Margaret.

"No," said Henry.

"Fine," said Margaret. "Susan! Bring me the scissors."

Susan ran off.

"Peter!" shouted Henry. "Worm! Lord

Worm! Lord High Worm!"

Peter stuck his head out of the upstairs window.

"Peter! Fetch the scissors! Quick!" ordered Henry.

"No," said Peter. "You fired me, remember?" And he slammed the window shut.

"You're dead, Peter," shouted Henry.

Sour Susan came back with the scissors and gave them to Margaret. Margaret held the scissors to Henry's flag. Henry didn't budge. She wouldn't dare –

Snip!

Aaargh! Moody Margaret cut off a corner of Henry's flag. She held the scissors poised to make another cut.

Horrid Henry had spent hours painting his beautiful flag. He knew when he was beat.

"Stop!" shrieked Henry.

He dropped Margaret's flag. Margaret dropped his flag. Slowly, they inched towards each other, then dashed to grab their own flag.

"Truce?" said Moody Margaret, beaming.

"Truce," said Horrid Henry, scowling.

I'll get her for this, thought Horrid Henry. No one touches my flag and lives.

★

Horrid Henry watched and waited until
it was dark and he heard the plinky-
plonk sound of Moody Margaret
practising her piano.

The coast was clear. Horrid Henry
sneaked outside, jumped over the wall
and darted inside the Secret Club Tent.

Swoop! He swept up the Secret Club
pencils and secret code book.

Snatch! He snaffled the Secret Club
stool.

Grab! He bagged the Secret Club
biscuit tin.

Was that everything?
No!

Scoop! He snatched the Secret Club motto ("Down with boys").

Pounce! He pinched the Secret Club carpet.

Horrid Henry looked around. The Secret Club tent was bare.

Except for –

Henry considered. Should he?

Yes!

Whisk! The Secret Club tent collapsed. Henry gathered it into his arms with the rest of his spoils.

Huffing and puffing, gasping and panting, Horrid Henry staggered off over the wall, laden with the Secret Club.

Raiding was hot, heavy work, but a pirate had to do his duty. Wouldn't all this booty look great decorating his fort? A rug on the floor, an extra biscuit tin, a repainted motto – "Down with girls" – yes, the Purple Hand Fort would have to be renamed the Purple Hand Palace.

Speaking of which, where was the Purple Hand Fort?

Horrid Henry looked about wildly for the Fort entrance.

It was gone.

He searched for the Purple Hand throne.

It was gone.

And the Purple Hand biscuit tin – GONE!

There was a rustling sound in the shadows. Horrid Henry turned and saw a strange sight.

There was the Purple Hand Fort leaning against the shed.

What?!

Suddenly the Fort started moving. Slowly, jerkily, the Fort wobbled across the lawn towards the wall on its four new stumpy legs.

Horrid Henry was livid. How dare someone try to nick his fort! This was an outrage. What was the world coming to, when people just sneaked into your garden and made off with your fort? Well, no way!

Horrid Henry let out a pirate roar.

"RAAAAAAAA!" roared Horrid Henry.

"AHHHHHHH!" shrieked the Fort.

CRASH!

The Purple Hand Fort fell to the ground. The raiders ran off, squabbling.

"I told you to hurry, you lazy lump!"

"You're the lazy lump!"

Victory!

Horrid Henry climbed to the top of his fort and grabbed his banner. Waving it proudly, he chanted his victory chant:

NAH NAH NE NAH NAH!

4

HORRID HENRY'S CAR JOURNEY

"Henry! We're waiting!"

"Henry! Get down here!"

"Henry! I'm warning you!"

Horrid Henry sat on his bed and scowled. His mean, horrible parents could warn him all they liked. He wasn't moving.

"Henry! We're going to be late," yelled Mum.

"Good!" shouted Henry.

"Henry! This is your final warning," yelled Dad.

"I don't want to go to Polly's!" screamed Henry. "I want to go to Ralph's birthday party."

Mum stomped upstairs.

"Well you can't," said Mum. "You're coming to the christening, and that's that."

"NO!" screeched Henry. "I hate Polly, I hate babies, and I hate you!"

Henry had been a page boy at the wedding of his cousin, Prissy Polly, when she'd married Pimply Paul. Now they had a prissy, pimply baby, Vomiting Vera.

Henry had met Vera once before. She'd thrown up all over him. Henry had hoped never to see her again until she was grown up and behind bars, but no such luck. He had to go and watch her be dunked in a vat of water, on the same day that Ralph was having a birthday party at Goo-Shooter World. Henry had been longing for ages to go to Goo-Shooter World. Today was his chance. His only chance. But no. Everything was ruined.

Perfect Peter poked his head round the door.

"*I'm* all ready, Mum," said Perfect Peter. His shoes were polished, his teeth were brushed, and his hair neatly combed. "I know how annoying it is to be kept waiting when you're in a rush."

"Thank you, darling Peter," said Mum. "At least one of my children knows how to behave."

Horrid Henry roared and attacked. He was a swooping vulture digging his claws into a dead mouse.

"AAAAAAAAAEEEEE!" squealed Peter.

"Stop being horrid, Henry!" said Mum.

"No one told me it was today!" screeched Henry.

"Yes we did," said Mum. "But you weren't paying attention."

"As usual," said Dad.

"*I* knew we were going," said Peter.

"I DON'T WANT TO GO TO POLLY'S!" screamed Henry. "I want to go to Ralph's!"

"Get in the car – NOW!" said Dad.

"Or no TV for a year!" said Mum.

Eeek! Horrid Henry stopped wailing. No TV for a year. Anything was better than that.

Grimly, he stomped down the stairs and out the front door. They wanted him in the car. They'd have him in the car.

"Don't slam the door," said Mum.

SLAM!

Horrid Henry pushed Peter away from the car door and scrambled for the right-

hand side behind the driver. Perfect
Peter grabbed his legs and tried to climb
over him.

Victory! Henry got there first.

Henry liked sitting on the right-hand
side so he could watch the speedometer.

Peter liked sitting on the right-hand
side so he could watch the speedometer.

"Mum," said Peter. "It's my turn to sit
on the right!"

"No it isn't," said Henry. "It's mine."

241

"Mine!"

"Mine!"

"We haven't even left and already you're fighting?" said Dad.

"You'll take turns," said Mum. "You can swap after we stop."

Vroom. Vroom.

Dad started the car.

The doors locked.

Horrid Henry was trapped.

But wait. Was there a glimmer of hope? Was there a teeny tiny chance? What was it Mum always said when he and Peter were squabbling in the car? "If you don't stop fighting I'm going to turn around and go home!" And wasn't home just exactly where he wanted to be? All he had to do was to do what he did best.

"Could I have a story tape please?" said Perfect Peter.

"No! I want a music tape," said Horrid Henry.

"I want 'Mouse Goes to Town'," said Peter.

"I want 'Driller Cannibals' Greatest Hits'," said Henry.

"Story!"

"Music!"

"Story!"

"Music!"

SMACK!

SMACK!

"Waaaaaa!"

"Stop it, Henry," said Mum.

"Tell Peter to leave me alone!" screamed Henry.

"Tell Henry to leave *me* alone!" screamed Peter.

"Leave each other alone," said Mum.

Horrid Henry glared at Perfect Peter.

Perfect Peter glared at Horrid Henry.

Horrid Henry stretched. Slowly, steadily, centimetre by centimetre, he spread out into Peter's area.

"Henry's on my side!"

"No I'm not!"

"Henry, leave Peter alone," said Dad. "I mean it."

"I'm not doing anything," said Henry. "Are we there yet?"

"No," said Dad.

Thirty seconds passed.

"Are we there yet?" said Horrid Henry.

"No!" said Mum.

"Are we there yet?" said Horrid Henry.

"NO!" screamed Mum and Dad.

"We only left ten minutes ago," said Dad.

Ten minutes! Horrid Henry felt as if they'd been travelling for hours.

"Are we a quarter of the way there yet?"

"NO!"

"Are we halfway there yet?"

"NO!!"

"How much longer until we're halfway there?"

"Stop it, Henry!" screamed Mum.

"You're driving me crazy!" screamed Dad. "Now be quiet and leave us alone."

Henry sighed. Boy, was this boring. Why didn't they have a decent car, with built-in video games, movies, and jacuzzi? That's just what he'd have, when he was king.

Softly, he started to hum under his breath.

"Henry's humming!"

"Stop being horrid, Henry!"

"I'm not doing anything," protested Henry. He lifted his foot.

"MUM!" squealed Peter. "Henry's kicking me."

"Are you kicking him, Henry?"

"Not yet," muttered Henry. Then he screamed.

"Mum! Peter's looking out of my window!"

"Dad! Henry's looking out of *my* window."

"Peter breathed on me."

"Henry's breathing loud on purpose."

"Henry's staring at me."

"Peter's on my side!"

"Tell him to stop!" screamed Henry and Peter.

Mum's face was red.

Dad's face was red.

"That's it!" screamed Dad.

"I can't take this anymore!" screamed Mum.

Yes! thought Henry. We're going to turn back!

But instead of turning round, the car screeched to a halt at the motorway services.

"We're going to take a break," said
Mum. She looked exhausted.

"Who needs a wee?" said Dad. He
looked even worse.

"Me," said Peter.

"Henry?"

"No," said Henry. He wasn't a baby.
He knew when he needed a wee and he
didn't need one now.

"This is our only stop, Henry," said
Mum. "I think you should go."

"NO!" screamed Henry. Several people

248

looked up. "I'll wait in the car."

Mum and Dad were too tired to argue. They disappeared into the services with Peter.

Rats. Despite his best efforts, it looked like Mum and Dad were going to carry on. Well, if he couldn't make them turn back, maybe he could *delay* them? Somehow? Suddenly Henry had a wonderful, spectacular idea. It couldn't be easier, and it was guaranteed to work. He'd miss the christening!

Mum, Dad, and Peter got back in the car. Mum drove off.

"I need a wee," said Henry.

"Not now, Henry."

"I NEED A WEE!" screamed Henry. "NOW!"

Mum headed back to the services.

Dad and Henry went to the toilets.

"I'll wait for you outside," said Dad. "Hurry up or we'll be late."

Late! What a lovely word.

Henry went into the toilet and locked the door. Then he waited. And waited. And waited.

Finally, he heard Dad's grumpy voice.

"Henry? Have you fallen in?"

Henry rattled the door.

"I'm locked in," said Henry. "The door's stuck. I can't get out."

"Try, Henry," pleaded Dad.

"I have," said Henry. "I guess they'll have to break the door down."

That should take a few hours. He

settled himself on the toilet seat and got out a comic.

"Or you could just crawl underneath the partition into the next stall," said Dad.

Aaargghh. Henry could have burst into tears. Wasn't it just his rotten luck to try to get locked in a toilet which had gaps on the sides? Henry didn't much fancy wriggling round on the cold floor. Sighing, he gave the stall door a tug and opened it.

Horrid Henry sat in silence for the rest of the trip. He was so depressed he didn't even protest when Peter demanded his turn on the right. Plus, he felt car sick.

Henry rolled down his window.

"Mum!" said Peter. "I'm cold."

Dad turned the heat on.

"Having the heat on makes me feel sick," said Henry.

"I'm going to be sick!" whimpered Peter.

"I'm going to be sick," whined Henry.

"But we're almost there," screeched Mum. "Can't you hold on until – "

Bleeeachh.

Peter threw up all over Mum.

Bleeeechhh. Henry threw up all over Dad.

The car pulled into the driveway. Mum and Dad staggered out of the

car to Polly's front
door.

"We survived,"
said Mum, mopping
her dress.

"Thank God that's
over," said Dad, mopping
his shirt.

Horrid Henry scuffed his feet sadly
behind them. Despite all his hard work,
he'd lost the battle. While Rude Ralph
and Dizzy Dave and Jolly Josh were dashing about spraying each other with green
goo later this afternoon he'd be stuck at a
boring party with lots of grown-ups yak
yak yaking. Oh misery!

Ding dong.

The door opened.
It was Prissy Polly.
She was in her
bathrobe and slippers.
She carried a stinky,

smelly, wailing baby over her shoulder. Pimply Paul followed. He was wearing a filthy T-shirt with sick down the front.

"Eeeek," squeaked Polly.

Mum tried to look as if she had not been through hell and barely lived to tell the tale.

"We're here!" said Mum brightly. "How's the lovely baby?"

"Too prissy," said Polly.

"Too pimply," said Paul.

Polly and Paul looked at Mum and Dad.

"What are you doing here?" said Polly finally.

"We're here for the christening," said Mum.

"Vera's christening?" said Polly.

"It's *next* weekend," said Paul.

Mum looked like she wanted to sag to the floor.

Dad looked like he wanted to sag beside her.

"We've come on the wrong day?" whispered Mum.

"You mean, we have to go and come back?" whispered Dad.

"Yes," said Polly.

"Oh no," said Mum.

"Oh no," said Dad.

"Bleeeach," vomited Vera.

"Eeeek!" wailed Polly.   "Gotta go." She slammed the door.

"You mean, we can go home?" said Henry. "Now?"

"Yes," whispered Mum.

"Whoopee!" screamed Henry. "Hang on, Ralph, here I come!"

HORRID HENRY'S NITS

Scratch. Scratch. Scratch. Horrid Henry has nits – and he's on a mission to give them to everyone else too. After that, he can turn his attention to wrecking the school trip, ruining his parents' dinner party, and terrifying Perfect Peter.

HORRID HENRY GETS RICH QUICK

(Originally published as *Horrid Henry Strikes It Rich*) Horrid Henry tries to sell off Perfect Peter and get rich, makes sure he gets the presents he wants for Christmas, sabotages Sports Day at school – and runs away from home.